THE MAN ON THE TRAIN

THE MAN ON THE TRAIN

A NOVEL OF SUSPENSE

DEBBIE BABITT

SCARLET
NEW YORK

THE MAN ON THE TRAIN

Scarlet
An Imprint of Penzler Publishers
58 Warren Street
New York, N.Y. 10007

First Scarlet Press edition

Interior design by Maria Fernandez

Library of Congress Control Number: 2023922352

ISBN: 978-1-61316-413-6
eBook ISBN: 978-1-61316-414-3

10 9 8 7 6 5 4 3 2 1

Printed in the United States of America
Distributed by W. W. Norton & Company

To Ted, as always
With love

Before you embark on a journey of revenge,
dig two graves.

—Confucius

I t was as if time had stopped when the body was dragged from the ocean.

The intervening years erased, the clock frozen on the moment that shattered the tranquility of their sleepy hamlet all those years ago.

Folks rushing to the beach the minute the news hit.

The onlookers gathering at the shoreline, awaiting their first glimpse of the victim, same as back then.

Not that everyone remembered.

Some folks had died. Or moved away. For those who remained, it was too long ago, and memory being what it is. Or never was.

Stories changed. People changed. What happened back then filtered through the distorted lens of grief.

Regret.

Anger.

And guilt.

Of course, there were differences between the two tragedies.

The time of year, for one thing.

Back in '84, it was one of those nights you waited for all summer.

Stars filling the sky. The moon casting a shimmering golden light on the ocean.

Waves lapping gently on the shore, a perfect backdrop to the most anticipated event of the season. The beach packed with people, mostly teenagers on the cusp of adulthood. They were among the first to reach the scene.

In contrast, tonight was dark and cold.

No stars in the leaden sky, a harbinger of the storm predicted to arrive tomorrow.

The holiday season had just ended, leaving everyone with nothing to look forward to but the rest of the long, bleak winter.

That didn't stop townsfolk from bundling up and coming out in droves, despite the inhospitable weather.

A hush fell over the crowd as the medical examiner made his lumbering way across the snow-covered sand. The same forensics expert who gave the official cause of death in the '84 case, now four decades older and slowed by arthritis and gout.

Gasps of recognition went up and down the beach when the water-logged corpse was laid on the sand and everyone got a look at the victim's face.

A face many thought they'd never see again.

Which only deepened the mystery and set minds racing about the meaning of this shocking turn of events.

Questions once again on everyone's lips.

Questions that had never been answered.

All these years later, no one really knew what happened up there.

The best anyone could say for sure was that when the night was over, somebody was dead.

And now death had claimed another one of their own.

The crowd parted to make way for the chief of police, who'd just pulled up in his four-wheel Jeep.

In 1984, he'd been a wet-behind-the-ears sergeant who many had thought was in over his head. Community outrage pressured him to make an arrest, and he lacked the experience to deal with a violent crime in what had always been a peaceful fishing paradise. Before then, the worst crime that summer was someone stealing a bicycle off of someone else's front porch.

A few pointed out that, in the same year, there was the tragedy of the four fishermen lost at sea after their boat went down, never to be found.

But that wasn't murder, at least as far as anyone knew. It wasn't the deliberate and savage snuffing out of the life of one human being by another.

The murder was never solved.

Depriving the town of justice.

And closure.

Leaving a black stain on their community.

As the medical examiner and the chief of police conferred over the corpse, a silent question rose up from the crowd.

Would this new tragedy finally bring resolution?

Or bury the truth forever?

PART I

PART I

Six Months Later . . .

1

The clanging in her ear was loud enough to wake the dead.

Except that he wasn't ever going to open his eyes again.

She was at the front of the church, the organ shrilling, the casket before her closed so that no one would have to see his broken bones.

But all she could think as she stood there in her Sunday best, grief squeezing the breath out of her chest, was that it was such a big coffin for such a small body.

The echoes of the organ faded as she came fully awake. Though a part of her was still back at the funeral.

She hadn't had that particular dream in a long time.

Linda reached up and grabbed her cell off the nightstand.

The tiny screen was dark.

It wasn't her phone.

The sound came again, reverberating through the house.

It was the front door.

She swiped her phone. When the screen lit up, she looked at the time.

A few minutes after six.

She hadn't slept later than four-thirty in years.

The bell pealed a third time. Louder. More insistent.

She shook off the last remnants of sleep.

Who the hell was invading their privacy this early on a Saturday morning?

She turned to her husband.

But Guy's solid form wasn't under the blanket with a pillow over his head, his way of blocking out the world.

His side of the bed was empty. The blanket was turned down, the sheets Guy often left in a tangle at the foot of the bed neatly tucked in with the hospital corners she unfailingly made each morning; a carryover from childhood. There wasn't even the slightest indentation in the pillow to indicate that his head had rested there.

Guy never came to bed last night.

She felt the first stirrings of alarm.

When she swung her legs over the side of the bed, the room spun. She took a breath, fought back a wave of nausea. As she reached for her robe, she forced her mind to replay last night's timeline.

When she pulled into the driveway, at a little before nine, the windows were dark.

Her first thought was that he'd gone to bed early.

The house was empty.

Maybe he'd gotten tired of having dinner by himself and gone out. It was date night, after all.

She'd spent most of the evening in an empty courtroom, standing before twelve vacant juror seats and practicing her summation, something she'd been doing since her early days at the Manhattan District Attorney's office.

So where was he?

The doorbell rang again.

Her heart beating erratically, Linda went to their bedroom window, which overlooked the front of the house, and peeked through the blinds.

There were two of them. A man and a woman.

In plain clothes, but she knew.

She was hit by a fresh wave of panic.

Police at the door never meant good news.

She ordered herself to calm down. But her brain didn't listen, her mind, as always, going to the dark place.

Something had happened to Guy.

As she slowly descended the stairs, she thought about all the ways it could have played out.

The most obvious was that he'd gotten into an accident on his way home from the train station. Another driver cut him off, which always infuriated Guy, and he fell victim to road rage. But that would have happened last night. Surely she would have been informed before now?

Unless—

On the bottom step, she stopped.

He wouldn't.

Would he?

All these years of watching him like a hawk, unable to take a relaxing breath until the date had passed.

Except that this year was different, wasn't it?

How could she have failed to see this coming? If Guy had done something terrible, it was her fault. All the late nights, knowing the pain and loss he was reliving.

What about her pain? Her loss?

Fragments of the dream sliced through her mind.

Did that matter now?

As she stepped into the entry hall, she thought she knew now how the families of victims felt.

She took a deep breath. Mentally tried to prepare herself. But how do you prepare for something like this?

With every nerve in her body screaming *Don't!*, she opened the door.

Two Weeks Earlier . . .

2

The 8:04 was pulling into the station.

When the train stopped, the lines of commuters surged forward in perfect synchronicity, gliding across the platform as one.

The same dance they'd been doing for decades.

Guy tucked his newspaper under his arm and hitched his book bag higher on his shoulder as he moved with the other passengers toward the train doors, giving a nod here and a smile there as he spied those who'd shared his daily ride for years. With a few, he was on a first-name basis, exchanging meaningless pleasantries. Usually about sports, a subject he couldn't care less about, despite his father's endless efforts to turn his only son into an athlete.

When the doors opened, it was every man and woman for themselves.

Once aboard the train, Guy was shocked to spot an open window seat. The coveted aisle seats were already gone of course, leg room at a premium aboard the early-morning express into Grand Central. A window was the next best thing, a hell of a lot better than the cramped middle seat where he'd been forced to sit on more than one occasion.

He moved quickly, elbowing his way past passengers on the hunt for seats until he reached the third row. The man in the aisle seat barely glanced up from his phone as Guy slid past, thinking as he had countless times before that people rarely communicated anymore. Knowing he was in the minority, out of touch with reality despite the fact that he often did the same thing to avoid having to engage. He usually found that having his head in a book or a newspaper in front of his face were just as effective and made him feel that he was doing his part to help stave off the demise of the printed page.

After Guy settled into his seat, he unfolded the newspaper and opened to the local section. He'd barely gotten through the first article when the words on the page started to blur together. He leaned back against the headrest.

At night, he'd fallen into the habit of staying up late reading in his study, only to startle awake, the book open in his lap.

After going upstairs and getting into bed, careful to not disturb his sleeping wife, he'd lie there. Heart pounding. Mind racing. Asking the profound, disturbing questions that seemed to plague him more and more lately and always seemed to come in the dead of night.

Like what the hell he was doing with his life.

Commuting every day to a job he'd begun to hate more and more. Feeling trapped. Wondering if this was it. All there was.

He heard the doors closing. As the train started to move, the motion of the wheels lulled him.

He felt his lids growing heavy.

His eyes drifted closed.

He was standing in front of a door. He wanted to move, but it was as if he were frozen in place.

"Excuse me."

Guy opened his eyes.

A woman was standing next to his row.

"Is this seat taken?"

She was indicating the middle seat, where Guy had tossed his book bag after settling in at the window. He murmured an apology and removed the offending bag, trying to shake off the last vestiges of sleep.

The man in the aisle seat—no longer glued to his phone—shifted his body to allow her to pass. Something he hadn't done for Guy. Why would he? As she settled into her seat, the man was still eying her in the way a man looks at an attractive woman.

She *was* attractive, in a red dress that set off her dark hair, which was swept back in a loose bun at the nape of her long neck.

Guy realized he was staring. He tried to cover his embarrassment by asking if she had enough room. Which was a stupid question given that she'd already lowered the armrest that separated their seats. She nodded, and he quickly glanced away. When he chanced a look back, the woman was rummaging in her bag and the man in the aisle seat had gone back to studying his phone.

Guy retreated once again behind his paper, but he was distracted. As the train picked up speed, he glanced at his own phone. He was surprised to see that fifteen minutes had passed since they'd left the station. More than half the ride was over.

He could have sworn he'd heard the doors closing as he started to nod off.

So where had the woman come from?

Another car. That must be it. She'd probably been moving from car to car until she found an empty seat.

Maybe she was new to commuting. Which made sense because he didn't recall having seen her before.

And she was someone he would have remembered.

She was sliding something from her bag.

It was a book. Not a device, but an honest-to-God physical book. Guy couldn't remember the last time he'd seen anyone reading an actual book on the train. Ironic, given what he did for a living. Out of habit, he craned his neck to see the name on the spine.

And received another pleasant jolt.

This wasn't just any book. With the exception of himself, he didn't know a single person who read the classics anymore.

As if sensing his gaze, she turned back to him.

Her eyes were a deep, dark brown, with golden flecks in the center.

"Have you read him before?" Guy asked.

She shook her head. "I have to admit, it's a bit of a slog. Maybe because I'm a slow reader. But I figured I had to start somewhere."

Guy nodded. "Dostoyevsky has always been one of my favorite authors. *Crime and Punishment* is his masterpiece. All that moral ambiguity. *The Brothers Karamazov* will give you a run for your money, although some find the story's theme of patricide is hard to take. After you finish reading this one, you should tackle *War and Peace*. Many believe Tolstoy was the greatest Russian writer who ever lived. Did you know he died at a train station?"

He paused for breath.

It occurred to him that she might prefer a female author.

He'd always been partial to Jane Austen.

And Virginia Woolf.

His mother's favorite.

The woman was looking at him.

"Sorry. I didn't mean to go on."

"I didn't mind." She cocked her head, a smile once again teasing at the corners of her lips.

Guy wondered if she was flirting.

"You must be a writer."

He should have seen that one coming.

After a long moment, he nodded.

It wasn't a lie. He did write for a living.

Even if he no longer lived to write.

"I'm impressed," she said. "I've never met a real writer."

Guy had no response for that. He waited for the inevitable next question.

Have you written anything I might have read?

Nothing that anyone would have read. He pictured the pile of unpublished manuscripts gathering dust in his attic.

"I could never write a novel." She smiled again, indicated the book that still lay unopen on her lap. "Tell me more about Dostoyevsky."

"Sure." Guy marveled at the dexterity with which she'd steered the conversation away from his failed writing career.

He started talking, warming once again to his favorite subject. He spoke about the themes in Dostoyevsky's novels. About retribution and guilt. About fathers murdered by their offspring. About tragedy and loss and suffering that were an inescapable component of the human condition.

She never interrupted as he spoke, her eyes fixed on him as if she were truly interested in what he had to say.

When the train pulled into Grand Central, they both rose from their seats at the same time. He hadn't realized how tall she was until he stood. She was only a few inches shorter than his five-foot-ten.

There was an awkward moment as they stood there. The commuter who'd sat in the aisle seat was already headed for the open doors.

The woman started to move out of the row, then turned back to Guy. "I enjoyed our conversation. I feel like I learned something. You really know your stuff."

He tried to shrug it off, but he felt a warm glow inside. "I've been reading the classics since I was a kid."

"I can tell." Her eyes were still on him. He found it hard to look away. For a crazy moment, it felt as if they were the only two people on the train.

She smiled, then turned and walked out of the row.

Guy followed her off the train and into the terminal. He was about to ask her name, but she was already moving past him.

Disappearing into the rush-hour throng.

3

W here the hell was it?

It was supposed to be on Track 110.

It was always on Track 110.

Guy raced back upstairs, scanned the board. And there it was: The 5:52 to North White Plains . . . Scarsdale . . . on Track 116.

He checked his phone as he ran back downstairs.

5:51.

Sixty seconds to make the train.

When he arrived at the track, the last few commuters were boarding. Guy couldn't believe his luck when he spied an aisle seat. He made a beeline for it, beating out another commuter with the same idea.

He deserved it after the day from hell he'd just had.

It wasn't as if he'd set out to deliberately hurt anyone. He didn't even realize he'd dozed off until his assistant gave him a sharp nudge in the ribs. He startled awake, disoriented and not sure where he was—the first time that had happened—until he saw the associate publisher glaring at him across the conference table.

After the meeting ended, his boss called him into her office, where she told him that this was his second warning.

He didn't remember getting the first.

As the train left Grand Central, Guy stretched out his legs and tried to relax. But he was still seething.

It had been demoralizing enough being passed over for promotion last month. He should have been the new marketing director. Not some entitled kid who'd been with the company a paltry five years. He should have been the one in the coveted corner office instead of his dark, depressing cave with its view of an air shaft.

After all the time and loyalty he'd given them, this was how they rewarded him?

He should quit. Something he should have done a long time ago.

The pocket of his jacket buzzed.

He must have forgotten to take his phone off vibrate when he left the office.

He slid it out.

There was a voicemail.

Linda was working late.

Again.

He knew what was really going on. It didn't matter that he hadn't missed a deadline in almost two decades, or that he had created successful ad campaigns for their biggest books.

At the ripe old age of fifty-six, he'd outlived his usefulness. He was irrelevant. Inconsequential.

A footnote in his own life.

Even his wife couldn't be bothered to have dinner with him.

"Hey, Guy."

He looked up. Across the aisle, a man was waving. It was Ralph Morris, an accountant who lived two houses down from him and was in love with the sound of his own voice. Guy felt trapped; a deer caught in the headlights. He didn't even have his newspaper to hide behind.

Morris didn't come up for air the entire ride, keeping up a steady stream of inane small talk that set Guy's teeth on edge.

When the train pulled into the station, Guy was the first one off. On the platform, he stopped so short another person rammed into him.

"Sorry," the man muttered.

Guy didn't answer. He was staring at someone who'd emerged from the last car.

It was the woman from the 8:04.

He'd had no idea that they shared the same evening commute. His mind returned to their conversation on the train this morning. Everything else—this whole nightmarish day—was wiped from his mind as he watched her hurry down the stairs.

She was headed in the direction of the taxi stand.

Which meant that she didn't have a car.

Guy wondered where she lived as he started walking. It had to be one of the three towns that fed into the Scarsdale line, all of which were within a twenty-minute ride of each other.

Should he offer her a lift?

Even if it cost him some extra time, did it matter? It wasn't as if he had anyone waiting for him at home. Just another night alone with the TV and reheated leftovers.

A driver had just gotten out of one of the cabs. He was holding open the passenger door.

Guy watched her get into the taxi.

Too late.

He'd missed his chance.

4

H e awoke to the pungent aroma of brewing coffee.
Despite a familiar feeling of exhaustion from another fitful
night, Guy threw off the blanket.

When he'd left the Scarsdale station last night, he'd felt restless and
unsettled, unable to bear the thought of another night alone. Instead
of driving home, he stopped at a local restaurant and ended up having
dinner at the bar.

Which only made him feel worse.

Next to him on neighboring stools were other solo patrons, several
of them making conversation with the bartender out of loneliness or
desperation. That depressed the hell out of him, and he felt a craving
he hadn't experienced in a long while. He left half his meal, eying the
bottles behind the bar as he paid his bill. He was about to call over
the bartender and order a shot, but he'd promised his wife.

And Guy took his promises seriously.

In the kitchen, Linda was standing at the stovetop with her back
to him.

Guy couldn't remember the last time his wife had cooked breakfast.

Most mornings, she was already dressed and packing up her brief-case when he came downstairs. She'd give him a quick kiss before heading out the door.

Lately, it felt more and more as if they were ships passing in the night. Two people who happened to live in the same house but no longer had anything in common.

Linda turned around when she heard him come in.

She looked especially pretty today in a powder-blue suit that matched her eyes.

"Sleep well?" she asked as she slid bacon and eggs onto two plates, the eggs over easy the way he liked them.

"Okay." The yawn he tried to stifle belied his response. He felt her eyes on him as he helped carry the plates and two steaming mugs to the table.

Last night, he'd been reading as usual when he heard her car pull into the garage. It was after nine, the latest she'd come home yet. Linda seemed preoccupied when she walked into the study, giving him a quick kiss good night and telling him not to stay up too late. As he listened to her upstairs getting ready for bed, his mind spun different scenarios.

He studied her across the table now as she sipped her tea, on the lookout for anything out of the ordinary.

There was the suit, for one thing. He didn't think he'd seen her wearing it before.

The blond hair she usually wore in a ponytail was loose today, flowing in soft waves to her shoulders.

She was wearing makeup.

And was that a new perfume?

"I'm sorry for all the late nights," she said, as if sensing his thoughts. "But you know how crazy it is when I'm on trial. Especially when I'm prepping witnesses. And they're usually not available until after the work day's over."

"I understand."

Did he? Now that he thought about it, he couldn't recall having spent so many nights alone before. In fact, in the not-too-distant past, Linda used to seek his advice, especially when she was writing her opening and closing statements to deliver to the jury.

Guy couldn't remember the last time she'd asked his advice. About anything.

"What's happening at work?" Linda asked as she folded her napkin on her lap.

"Nothing special."

She didn't say anything. What response could she give? He put down his coffee and started eating. But he could feel her censure. Feel her judging him.

She knew about the promotion that had never materialized. Had shared his disappointment and commiserated with him at the time. Now what was he supposed to tell her? Not only was it doubtful that he'd ever advance any further, but he was probably going to end up getting fired.

While his wife's star was rising, his had fallen several leagues below sea level.

He didn't tell her any of that. The last thing he needed was her pity.

They ate in silence. Not the companionable silence they used to share, but one that felt fraught with things unsaid.

After almost thirty years of marriage, that was a motherlode.

"Guy."

He knew that tone. Had he done something wrong? Failed once again to meet her expectations? An errand he forgot? A chore he'd neglected to do? Maybe it was his imagination, but lately it seemed as if she was critical of everything he did.

"You don't have to keep working there, you know. You could—"

"Do what? Look for another job? Who's going to hire me at my age?" He put down his fork. He'd lost his appetite.

"I was just—I only meant—" She shook her head. He'd rarely seen her at a loss. She was always the commanding, in-control prosecutor. She lowered her voice, almost as if she were apologizing. "Maybe you could start writing again."

Guy stared at her. Was she out of her mind?

He hadn't written anything in years.

That train had come and gone.

"Can we please change the subject?"

"It's not as if we need the money."

Another blow to his ego and what was left of his manly pride. "And let my wife support me?"

"Forget it. I'm sorry I brought it up."

So was he.

Another silence fell.

He pushed away the plate of half-eaten food his wife had gone to the trouble to prepare. And instantly regretted his sharp words.

"I'm sorry, Linda."

"I was only trying to help. I just wanted to make sure you're—that everything's okay."

Now he understood. It was because of the approaching anniversary. This was the time to tell her that he was having the dream again. But that would only make her worry more. And she had her own issues.

"I'm fine." He gave her what he hoped was a reassuring smile. "How's the trial going?" He figured that was a safe topic, one his wife always enjoyed talking about.

Because she loved her work. Unlike him.

Her eyes searched his face, as if she didn't believe him. Then she picked up her mug of tea, frowned because it had gone cold. "We've got six more witnesses before the case goes to the defense. Defendant's going to take the stand. Not that it's going to make a difference. There's too much evidence against him. I don't think there's a single juror who believes he didn't do it."

"Do you ever wonder if they're innocent?"

This was a discussion they used to have frequently. And one reason he wasn't completely enamored with what his wife did for a living.

"Not a chance," she said now. "Speaking of which, I'd better get going."

Guy helped her clear the table, then loaded the dishes and cutlery into the dishwasher while she got her things together.

After they'd kissed goodbye and Linda left the house—she really did look especially attractive this morning—suspicion once again reared its ugly head.

That would explain the late nights. The distance he felt between them.

He thought about their conversation at breakfast. The things left unspoken.

Like the fact that maybe she was tired of having a failure for a husband.

Hadn't he caught her looking at him sometimes, seen his lack of achievement reflected in her eyes? Remembering how, once upon a time, he'd read aloud to her from the current novel he was writing. On his way to becoming his generation's next modern classicist.

He'd been deceiving himself.

But if his wife really was having an affair—he felt a stab of jealousy at an unwelcome image of that PI who worked with her—wouldn't he have sensed it before now?

Or was it true that the husband was always the last to know?

5

The train was pulling into the station when Guy drove up an hour later.

And the lot was full.

He could park on the street, but then he'd risk getting a ticket.

Did he have a choice? He couldn't be late. Not after his boss had given him two warnings.

Three strikes and you're out.

He was sorry he hadn't handed in his resignation yesterday. But then he'd have to look for another job. He'd meant what he'd said at breakfast this morning. No way was he living off of his wife.

That would be the death knell for his marriage.

After Linda left this morning, he'd gone downstairs into the finished section of the basement that his wife had converted into her home office. He went through her desk, searching for proof that she was having an affair. He didn't know what he expected to find and again felt guilty for his suspicions. By the time he realized he was on a fool's errand, it was later than he'd realized.

The train doors had opened.

The lines of commuters were moving up.

Now he'd have to take his chances and pray that no traffic cops came by.

His car keys jingled in his hand as he sprinted for the train. Why was he still holding them? Did he forget to put them away? Or forget to lock the car?

He glanced over his shoulder as he ran.

A car with the familiar *Scarsdale Traffic* logo was pulling up next to his.

He turned back to the train.

The last few commuters were getting on.

As he ran, he weighed his options. Missing his train versus the cost of the ticket.

No contest.

He looked back.

The cop was getting out of his car.

He ran up the stairs leading to the platform, still looking over his shoulder—*Fuck the ticket!*—and barreled into someone.

She stumbled back, her bag sliding from her shoulder.

"I'm so sorry," Guy said. "Are you—"

He stopped midsentence. He felt as if the wind had been knocked out of him.

It was her.

The woman from the train.

"Hi, again. No, it's my fault. I was late and—uh-oh. Guess we'd better make a run for it." She looked at him as she secured her bag over her shoulder. "Are you coming?"

The train doors were closing.

And then they were running, side by side, making it aboard with seconds to spare.

6

They stood in the well by the doors, swaying a little with each movement of the train.

The woman turned to look at him. "I thought yesterday was bad. But today." She shook her head. "Is it always this crowded?"

Guy nodded. "Especially the eight-oh-four. Especially midweek. And a lot of people get on at Scarsdale."

"Guess I'm going to have to get here earlier."

He remembered how she'd come into his car looking for a seat yesterday morning. So he'd been right about her. "You just started commuting?"

"Guess it shows, huh? How about you? Doing this a long time?"

"Too long." Almost twenty-nine years, he realized with something of a shock, starting with his first job at a small, family-owned publishing house.

"I'm starting to know what you mean."

"It's not so bad." Guy couldn't believe he was defending his daily commute. "But you need a plan."

"A plan?"

"If you want a seat. Like everything, there's an art to it. The eight-oh-four is the most popular time, as you can see. Express all the way from here to Grand Central. You miss the train, you have to get the eight twenty local. Adds at least fifteen minutes to the ride. The next express isn't until eight thirty-six. So the first thing you have to do is get here at a quarter of. Not five of, not ten of. Not even twelve of.

"That's not all," Guy went on. "The other important piece of the puzzle is *where* you stand. You've seen those clusters of commuters all up and down the platform? They're standing there for a reason. It's where the doors open, depending which train you're waiting for. For example, for the eight-oh-four, you have to stand about a foot to the left of where you'd stand for the eight thirty-six. There's nothing on the platform to indicate it, you have to go by experience. If you want two seats together, you have to get here even earlier. And that's not all. You have to stand in a specific place if you want a particular car. For instance, on my morning commute, I always sit in the first car. But for the five fifty-two back to Scarsdale, it's the last car. It's been my routine for years."

He watched her face when he mentioned the 5:52, but she didn't react. Maybe she hadn't seen him in the parking lot last night.

"Sounds like a lot of moving parts," she said.

"It's not as complicated as it sounds. Once you get it down."

She nodded, cocked her head. "I'll try to remember."

The train rocked again. Her hip brushed his thigh.

Guy was barely aware of time passing. It could have been minutes. Hours.

The train started to pick up speed.

They were approaching the tunnel.

Seconds later, the lights went out.

Guy could no longer see her as the train thundered toward Grand Central.

When the lights came back on, he blinked at the sudden brightness. The doors screeched open.

The woman hitched her bag higher on her shoulder and started to move toward the open doors. Then stopped, as if she'd just thought of something. "By the way, I'm Anna."

It was the perfect name for her. The name of one of his favorite fictional heroines.

In fact, he'd recently finished rereading the novel, much of it during his daily commute.

She was looking at him, and he realized he hadn't responded. "Guy," he finally said.

Anna smiled. "Nice to meet you, Guy. And thanks for the commuting tips."

He started to follow her toward the exit, but a passenger in the row opposite blocked his way. By the time he disembarked, the platform was a crush of people.

It was just as crowded in the terminal, but he spotted the blue dress she was wearing as she walked toward the Lexington Avenue exit.

He glanced at the big clock in the middle of Grand Central. He'd better get a move on.

Still he stood there, his gaze once again sliding to the exit.

She was gone.

7

That night, Guy went over to the bookcase against the far wall in the living room, where the books were arranged alphabetically by author.

Now that he knew Anna shared a literary sisterhood with her namesake, Anna Karenina, he thought Tolstoy's most famous novel would be the ideal book to introduce her to after she finished the Dostoyevsky.

Reading the classics was a task he'd first set for himself when he was a lonely, unhappy teenager. Many of the books were part of the collection he'd inherited from his mother.

His gaze slid to the empty space on the bottom shelf.

That particular novel by Virginia Woolf had been missing for decades.

Guy figured he'd loaned it to someone and the book was never returned.

8

When he walked onto the platform Thursday morning, Anna was already in line, holding a place for him.

Guy quickened his pace, feeling a surge of pleasure at the sight of her.

The train was pulling in as he reached the line of commuters. Anna was third from the front. She waved when he approached.

"Good morning, Guy."

"Hello, Anna."

He liked saying her name.

After they boarded, Guy spotted two aisle seats in opposite rows. Anna had seen them too and, as if by unspoken agreement, they each took a seat so they were across from one another.

When the train left the station, she reached into her bag. He couldn't resist sneaking a peek at her book to see how far she'd progressed.

The bookmark appeared to be in approximately the same place it had been the other day. No one ever said reading the classics was easy, but he admired her for making the effort.

On the other hand, *Anna Karenina* should make for easier reading.

As the train rumbled along the tracks, he imagined introducing Anna to all the wonderful novels that had made him decide to become a writer.

He felt eyes on him.

Across the aisle, Anna was watching him. When their eyes met, she smiled.

Then she returned her attention to her book.

9

Guy arrived as the 5:52 was coming down the tracks.

The evening train was always less crowded, a little past the rush hour, and he found a seat in the last car easily.

He looked around for Anna.

She made it aboard just as the doors started to close.

When she reached his row, Guy rose to his feet. The cars on the 5:52 were narrower, with only two seats across. The window seat next to his aisle seat was empty.

"We really have to stop meeting like this," she said with a teasing smile.

After Anna was settled in the window seat, they made small talk for a few minutes. Typical back-and-forth on safe, neutral topics like the traffic and, of course, the weather—unusually warm for late May—that he'd somehow thought they'd moved beyond.

As they talked, his mind buzzed with questions he knew he had no business asking.

He, of all people, was aware of the number-one unspoken rule of commuting: never get personal.

Anna must have sensed the direction of his thoughts because she'd stopped talking.

An awkward silence fell.

When she pulled her book out, Guy took his cue and slipped in his earbuds. But as the sounds of a distant trumpet filled his ears, he found his gaze sliding over to the window seat.

Today Anna was wearing a high-necked, black-and-white dress that ended at midcalf and flattered her long, slender curves. He'd taken note of her attire that morning on the Scarsdale platform.

So far, he hadn't seen her in a suit.

The ring finger of her left hand was bare.

He wondered if she had a boyfriend.

What kind of job she commuted to on a daily basis.

Who she was when she wasn't on the train.

She lifted her head.

Had she caught him staring?

Embarrassed, he turned away. After a minute or two, he leaned back and listened to music for the rest of the ride.

When the train pulled into the station, he waited for her to precede him out of the row. Then he followed her onto the platform and down the steps. They said goodnight in the parking lot.

She was halfway to the taxi stand when he called her name.

Her walking slowed. He wasn't sure if he saw her hesitate before turning around.

"Can I give you a lift?" he asked.

After a long moment during which Guy could swear he stopped breathing, she finally said, "That would be great." She took a step toward him, then stopped. "You sure? I don't want to take you out of your way."

He told her that he wouldn't be going out of his way at all.

10

Anna was quiet as they pulled out of the lot.

As he drove, Guy wondered what she was thinking. He was sure now that she didn't live alone. A woman that attractive had to have a significant other in her life.

She still hadn't said a word when he approached the center of town. It was busy for a midweek evening. Lots of people milling on the street. He was about to ask her where she lived when she finally spoke.

"You can drop me here. I think I'll stay in town a while. Maybe stop for a quick drink. Thanks for the lift."

"Mind if I join you?"

One of her beautifully sculpted brows lifted. She looked as surprised as he felt. As their gazes held, he became aware that he'd just crossed a line. She was aware of it too.

A part of him wished he could take the words back. The jury might still be out on whether his wife was faithful, but that was no excuse for him to spend time with another woman.

He could still get out of it. Tell Anna that he'd forgotten there was somewhere he had to be and ask if he could he take a raincheck.

Or maybe she'd save him the trouble of lying by turning him down. Could be she was meeting someone and had couched her words in a way to make him think she was a woman on her own. Which would serve him right for asking in the first place.

"I wouldn't mind at all."

In the passenger seat, where only his wife had ever sat, Anna leaned forward. Craned her long, swan-like neck as she looked out the window. "We're in luck. There's a spot."

11

T he place was packed.

Guy had driven past the bar dozens of times but had never gone inside. When Anna chose it, he figured she knew the place.

Not that that was any of his business.

Practically standing room only; every bar seat taken. The music coming through the speakers pounded in his ears as Guy elbowed his way through the happy-hour crowd to the table Anna had spotted in the back.

When he got there, he was aware of the admiring glances directed her way.

It had been a long time since he'd experienced that particular testosterone thing unique to the male of the species, and he basked in the knowledge that other men envied him being seen in the company of a beautiful woman.

Anna seemed oblivious to the attention as Guy set down a glass of house red in front of her. Anna indicated to his glass. "What are you drinking?"

"Club soda with a twist."

To her credit, she didn't ask why his drink was nonalcoholic.

There was a very good reason.

He became a different person when he had a few drinks in him.

Angry. Mean. Abusive.

Just like his father.

And he'd promised his wife.

Thinking about Linda sent guilt coursing through him. He tried to ignore it as he sat across from Anna.

It was quieter here, at the back of the bar. It made Guy feel as if he and Anna were on their own island, apart from the rest of the world.

It felt exciting.

And dangerous.

He watched her sip her wine, and when she put down the glass, he leapt into the breach. "Come here often?"

He'd meant it as a joke. A riff on the classic pickup line. Partially to cover his nervousness and partially to avoid thinking about what he was really doing here.

And hoping that she might reveal something about herself.

Anna cocked her head. "To be honest, I don't usually do this. Have drinks with strange men."

Her light, teasing tone matched his. It also gave him the perfect opening to ask her something personal. Like who was the special man in her life.

Her gaze shifted to his left hand, where the gold of his wedding band winked in the dim light of the sconces mounted on the walls.

She knew he was married.

Of course she did. Although he'd never actually come out and said it—they barely knew each other, after all—he hadn't tried to keep his marital status a secret.

Now was the moment to tell her about Linda. To let her know that he didn't do this sort of thing either.

But the words died in his throat. After their glasses were empty, he rose to his feet and offered to get another round.

"Only if you join me."

Guy looked down at her.

Her expression was still playful.

But her voice held a challenge.

He slowly wended his way back to the bar.

"What can I get you?"

A bartender who looked like a female bodybuilder and sported an incongruous-looking heart tattoo on her massive upper right arm stood there.

"A glass of house red," Guy said. "And a club soda with a twist." He watched another bartender pouring from a familiar-looking bottle. "And a shot of Jack Daniels."

Just one, he told himself. What could one shot hurt?

Linda didn't have to know. Just as he didn't know what she was doing tonight.

And how could he let a woman drink alone?

When he returned to the table and they were once again sitting across from one another, Anna held up her wine glass.

Guy looked at the club soda, then picked up the shot glass.

Anna smiled as they clinked glasses. "To meeting on the train."

"To meeting on the train," Guy repeated as he tossed back the shot.

12

They met that night.
And the next.

And the night after that.

They always went to different bars.

Guy no longer looked for Anna on the platform each morning while he waited for the 8:04. By unspoken agreement, they sat in separate cars.

It was the same on the 5:52.

They waited until the other commuters had gotten into their cars and driven off and they were left alone together in the parking lot.

He reveled in the clandestine aspect of their encounters, anticipation of the evening ahead helping him get through the interminable day at work.

He loved having a secret life.

He was careful to keep his alcohol down to one drink. Two, tops. He knew his limit.

Sometimes, as they sat together—always at a table in the back—he didn't feel the need to say a word. When they did talk, they stuck to safe topics—films they'd seen, restaurants they liked.

And, of course, books.

He felt like a new man. Energized. Motivated. Capable of conquering the world.

He even had the crazy idea that he'd start writing again.

If Johnny Walker had something to do with his new lease on life and the fact that he was sleeping better—no dreams now disturbing his slumber—he didn't care.

Also by unspoken agreement, they didn't discuss their personal lives. When the guilt started to creep in, Guy would tell himself that he wasn't doing anything wrong. They were just fellow commuters sharing an innocent a drink (or two) before heading back to their regular lives.

Whenever his curiosity got the better of him and he subtly attempted to steer the conversation around to her, she would deflect and change the subject.

At times, in the dimness of the bar, it seemed to him that her face changed, her eyes becoming unreadable. He'd feel something emanating from her then, a kind of kinetic energy that belied her charming, casual demeanor and hinted at deeper, darker emotions.

One night, as he headed back to the bar for another round, something made him turn around.

At their table, Anna's head was down.

He watched her, struck by the stillness of her body. She barely moved a muscle as she stared into her glass. It was as if her body had gone to sleep. As if she'd disappeared somewhere deep inside herself, leaving only the outer shell.

Guy shook off his fanciful thoughts—probably the after-effects of the Scotch.

When she looked up and saw him, her face changed, her features animating once more.

Then she smiled the smile that was meant for him alone.

And she was Anna again.

Yesterday . . .

13

On Friday morning, a week after they'd started meeting, Guy was walking across Grand Central toward the subway.

Last night, he'd taken *Anna Karenina* down from the bookcase. It would be his gift to Anna.

Something passed through his mind just then, gone before he could catch it.

He was so deep in thought trying to retrieve the quicksilver memory that at first he didn't hear the footsteps behind him.

When Guy turned around, Anna was standing there. He knew instantly that something was wrong.

It wasn't just that they always made sure their paths didn't cross on the 8:04 or here in Grand Central. She seemed tense; jittery. Her hands never stopped moving.

"Anna, are you okay?" Guy asked in alarm.

"I—" She shook her head. In their short time together, he'd never seen her at a loss. "I just wanted to tell you. I won't be on the five fifty-two tonight."

"Why not?"

"I moved out. I should have done it months ago."

"Is everything all right?" A stupid question; it was obvious that it wasn't. He also knew he was treading into taboo personal territory.

She didn't answer, just cocked her head in that way he found so irresistible. Then she smiled. But it wasn't the charming, confident smile that had first attracted him.

It was as if he were seeing the woman behind the façade.

Frightened.

Angry.

Sad.

"I hope so," she finally said. "I have to go now. Can you meet me in the city tonight? Is five-thirty good?"

His mind raced. Linda was working late again. In some ways, meeting in the city made his life easier. Afterward, he could catch a later train and still make it home in plenty of time before his wife.

"Sure," Guy said. "Do you have a place in mind?"

"There's a bar on the corner of Hudson and West Houston Streets. Not far from where you work. See you then."

She started to turn to leave, looked nervously around.

Guy followed her glance, but all he saw was the usual horde of commuters hurrying through the terminal.

Then she walked away.

It seemed as if he was always watching her walk away.

He watched until he could no longer see her, until she once again vanished into the rush-hour crowd.

14

The late June sun was still high in the sky when Guy left his office at a little past five.

Instead of walking east to the subway, he headed in the opposite direction.

At the corner of Lafayette and Houston, he continued west, toward the Hudson River and a part of the city he rarely visited. When he reached Hudson Street, Guy spotted the bar immediately.

Anna was right. It was only a few blocks from his office.

As he crossed the street, it occurred to him that he didn't recall telling her where he worked. But then, his memory wasn't always that reliable when he was drinking.

Inside the bar, deafening music pumped through the speakers. After he'd accustomed his eyes to the dimness, he looked around.

This crowd was very different from the patrons of the upscale suburban bars that he and Anna usually patronized. The men and women here weren't your typical commuter happy-hour group. The place was filled with bikers and hard-looking women in tight skirts and high boots.

What his wife called the "rough trade."

Guy managed to snag two seats together at the bar. While he was waiting, he motioned over the bartender and ordered a shot.

By the time he'd tossed down the second shot, it was quarter to six. She was late.

He was starting to get worried, and he cursed himself for not getting her phone number. But that was part of the deal.

"Hey."

Guy turned around.

A man with a shaved head wearing a black bomber jacket stood there.

"You can't save seats." He pointed to Guy's bag on the adjacent bar stool.

"I'm waiting for someone," Guy said.

"You deaf? I said. You. Can't. Save. Seats."

"Says who?"

"Says me."

Guy shook his head and waved down the bartender again.

The man was still there when the bartender brought his drink, and Guy deliberately ignored him as he reached for his glass. The other man's arm shot out, sending the whiskey sloshing all over the bar.

"You just spilled my drink," Guy said.

"So?"

"Now you have to buy me another one."

"Who the hell do you think you're messing with?"

"Fuck you!"

"Fuck you!"

The man grabbed his arm, and Guy saw red.

He shook off the other man as if he were an annoying fly. Then he reared back and swung his arm. Before his fist could connect with the man's jaw, someone grabbed him from behind.

Guy tried to wrench away, but he was being held in a vise.

When the bartender finally let him go, Guy whirled around, ready to give him a piece of his mind. But the room spun, and he had to grab the edge of the bar for support.

It must have been that last shot.

"You're drunk. And I don't like you disturbing my patrons. Now get out of here before I call the cops."

Guy couldn't believe it. Why was he telling *him* to go? He wasn't the one who started this. He felt eyes on him and turned to see that a small crowd had gathered.

The man with the shaved head was smiling.

Guy felt rage reignite. All he wanted to do was wipe that shit-eating grin off his face.

The onlookers were staring, waiting to see what he was going to do. The bartender had pulled out his phone.

With as much dignity as he could muster, Guy slid out his wallet and tossed down some bills, and with one last murderous look at the man with the shaved head, he picked up his book bag.

He was looking for the way out of this hellhole when he heard someone call his name.

Guy squinted. Somehow, he'd ended up by the restrooms next to the rear exit. It was all shadows back here, but he could see Anna clearly.

"I've been waiting for you." His words slurred together.

"I know. I'm sorry."

"What's going on?"

"I'm so afraid."

"Of what?"

"The man I live with. Last night, I knew I had to do something."

"Why?" Her words were starting to break through his drunken haze. Her face looked so pale in the dimness. And was that a bruise under her left eye? "Did he hurt you?"

She nodded. "It's not the first time."

He had a sudden memory of the high-necked dress she'd been wearing on the 5:52.

The night he asked to join her for a drink.

Since that first night, hadn't he seen the fear in her eyes in unguarded moments? The way she would suddenly look over her shoulder?

How could he have missed the signs?

He of all people?

Or had he chosen to ignore them? Because he wanted to be with her so badly.

"Have you gone to the police?"

She shook her head. "I'm too scared. He said if I went to the police or tried to leave, he'd kill me."

Suddenly, Guy was wide-awake.

He saw himself at fifteen. It was a night the year before his mother died.

The abuse had escalated, but his mother refused to go to the police. Even after Guy packed both their suitcases, she was too afraid to leave.

He told her that this was their only chance.

The car arrived a few minutes later, but it wasn't the taxi he'd called. It was his father, who'd come home from court early.

That night, after he beat Guy and his mother, Louis Kingship warned them that if they ever tried to leave again, he'd kill them both.

Two women had just come out of one of the restrooms. Guy waited until they walked away before speaking again.

"Where is he now?" he asked Anna.

"I don't know. But I'm afraid he might have found out where I'm staying."

"Where's that?"

"I took a room in a hotel. I've got to go. I probably shouldn't have come here. I can't involve you in this."

"It's too late." He was already involved. "Where's the hotel?"

When she didn't answer, he said, "Anna, please. You've got to let me help you."

As he talked, Guy felt his hands ball into fists. He'd be damned if he was going to let this man go on hurting her.

She looked at him; seemed to make up her mind. "Okay. Give me your number. I'll call if I need you."

"By then it could be too late."

"Maybe I can find a way to reason with him." But her expression was doubtful. "And if he sees you, he might go ballistic. He's insanely jealous. What's your number?"

Her hand shook as she typed his cell number into her phone.

"Anna, promise you'll call the minute you see him. I'll be right here. I'm not going anywhere."

But she was already out the door.

15

The minutes ticked by.

Guy hadn't felt this helpless since he was a teenager.

He had no idea where Anna was staying. The hotel had to be in the area; it was probably why she'd chosen this bar. He slid out his phone and was Googling hotels in the area when his phone vibrated in his hand.

A call was coming in from an unknown number.

"Hello?"

"Guy?"

"Anna? Are you okay?"

She was talking, but he heard a lot of static on the line.

"Are you at the hotel?" he asked.

"Yes."

"Did you see him?"

"I'm not sure. I'm scared." She started crying. "I'm sorry."

"You have nothing to be sorry about."

"I feel so alone."

"Do you want me to come there?"

"Would you? I'd feel so much better."

"What's the address?"

She gave it to him. "Moonrise Hotel. Second floor. Room 2601. And Guy? Hurry."

Then the line went dead.

16

The Moonrise Hotel was a dump located around the corner from the bar, sandwiched between a pawn shop and a bodega halfway down the block, on the north side of the street.

When Guy peered through the glass-topped front door, the hotel's sorry excuse for a lobby was empty.

That didn't mean Anna was out of danger. The man could be upstairs by now. Easy to slip past the pimply kid at the front desk, who didn't look up from his computer screen as Guy headed for the stairs.

It occurred to Guy as he checked the stairwell that he had nothing to use if he had to confront Anna's abuser.

How would he protect her?

He hadn't been able to protect his mother, who lived in fear until the day she died.

No one was hiding in the stairwell.

When Guy emerged on the second floor, everything seemed eerily quiet. The only sound was the rasp of his own breathing.

Room 2601 was at the end of the hall, next to a grimy window that let out onto a rusty, decrepit-looking fire escape.

No one was out there.

Guy stopped in front of the door.

"Anna?"

There was no sound from within.

He reached out his hand.

The door swung open.

Today . . .

17

Linda stared at the two officers standing on her front porch.

The male cop spoke first. "Trent Locke," he said. "And this is Inga Russell." He showed Linda his badge.

NYPD. Which meant that whatever happened had been in the city, or it would be the Scarsdale PD at her door.

Linda knew many of the cops who worked out of One Police Plaza in Manhattan, so this had obviously been a top brass decision. Better to have the tragic news delivered by officers she didn't interact with on a daily basis.

She looked from one to the other, her mind taking notes. Like the fact that Locke, a tall man with an old-fashioned handlebar mustache, had at least a decade on Inga Russell, who had red hair, green eyes, and was clearly a rookie. She tried to read into their expressions, but like all good cops, they maintained their poker faces.

"Linda Kingship?"

Detective Locke—an alpha if she ever saw one—had a deep, vaguely threatening voice that no doubt worked well on unforthcoming suspects.

Then she realized that he'd addressed her by her married name. Not Linda Haley, executive assistant district attorney at the Manhattan DA's office.

Linda Kingship.

The victim's wife.

If she hadn't been sure before, she was now.

She nodded, her mouth not able to form words. Locke looked even taller as he straightened up from his slightly slouched position, his hands flexing and unflexing. He was the one who'd kept his finger depressed on the doorbell.

She took an instant dislike to him.

"May we come in?"

Detective Russell looked almost apologetic as she asked the question Linda herself had asked on occasions when she'd accompanied the police to the homes of families. Hope died when she heard those four fraught words.

The cops always said it was the worst part of the job.

They were waiting for her answer. She knew it was cowardly, but she didn't care.

She didn't invite them in. She'd rather hear the news out here.

The detectives looked at one another. No one said anything for several seconds, but Linda was sure they could hear the pounding of her heart.

Then Detective Locke did something strange. Through the door she'd left ajar, he tried to look past her, into the house.

"Is your husband home?"

At first, she wasn't sure that she'd heard him right. When it finally dawned that they hadn't come to tell her Guy was dead, she was hit by another curve ball.

They were looking for him.

Why?

Determined to keep her counsel and maintain the upper hand even as her mind raced with questions, Linda drew herself up to her own full height—five foot six. Then, instead of answering their question, she decided to force their hand by posing one of her own.

"Why do you want to know?" she asked in the commanding voice that cowed defense witnesses and had earned the respect of judges.

"We need to talk to him. Clear up any misunderstanding."

Linda had heard that one before. It was another typical police tactic. Telling a bald-faced lie in order to persuade a suspect to give up the ghost.

But she wasn't a typical suspect. Or a typical suspect's wife.

Locke took a step toward her. Linda stood her ground.

"We can come back with a warrant."

Another ploy designed to intimidate and instill fear.

She knew better. Even if they had probable cause, getting an arrest warrant took time. A detective had to sign a sworn affidavit. Then someone from the DA's office had to get a judge to sign off. And it wasn't yet six-thirty on a weekend morning.

What she was in the dark about was the crime they believed Guy guilty of committing. Defendants were always deemed guilty before a trial even started. And ninety-nine percent ended up convicted.

She'd always liked those odds, been proud of her role in helping to secure the convictions.

Linda turned to Detective Russell, clearly the good cop to her male counterpart's bad cop. "You want to tell me what this is about?"

Russell hesitated and glanced at her partner. No help there. She must have taken pity on Linda because she said, "There's been an incident."

Standard police-speak. That could refer to anything from jumping a turnstile to mass murder.

"What kind of incident?"

Before she could answer, Locke jumped in. "Is he here?" His voice and manner now openly belligerent.

Linda felt her own temper flare. "You know what? You can come back when you have a warrant."

She turned on her heel and went into the house, then slammed the door in his face.

18

"**Y**ou want to tell me what the hell's going on?"

On the other end, Linda could hear her breathing. No doubt debating the best way to play this. "He's my husband, for god's sake!"

"And you work for us," her boss finally said. "Look at it from my vantage point. Which you'd be doing if you weren't so close to this. Thinking rationally instead of letting your emotions get the better of you. Then you might understand."

Understand?

If Diane Moorland were in front of her right now, she would have happily throttled her.

"You could have had someone from the DA's office call. Asked Guy to come down. Handled this quietly. Civilly. Instead, you send the police to my home. Detectives I don't even know. Like I was the wife of some low-life criminal!"

"Which is precisely why we had to do it that way. Because of who you are. I'm sorry for that, Linda. I truly am. But you know as well as

I that we have to be very careful here. Make sure we dot all our *I*s and cross all our *T*s. The office can't be perceived as showing special favors."

Especially in an election year.

"All I'm asking is for you to cooperate. You didn't let the detectives into your home, which is your right. But we have no way of knowing whether Guy is there or not. And you know how this could play out. You'd be charged with harboring a fugitive. None of us want that to happen. The sooner we can talk to Guy, the better it will be for him. For all of us."

Her voice was maddeningly calm, which only stoked Linda's anger.

"Why do you want to talk to him? What do you think Guy's done?"

In the background, Linda heard the voice of Diane's assistant, Terence. She pictured her boss behind her imposing mahogany desk in her corner office with the spectacular city view at One Hogan Place.

She could count on the fingers of one hand the number of times Diane had left her Connecticut mansion on a weekend to come to work. Let alone called in her assistant. Now Linda could hear papers being shuffled, documents bearing the official seal of the Manhattan District Attorney's office.

Documents that no doubt also bore her husband's name.

On the other end, Diane let out one of her long-suffering sighs. "You're going to know soon enough. Better you hear it from me. Someone was murdered last night."

Linda's stomach did a three-sixty.

She tasted the ham and cheese sandwich she'd hastily consumed yesterday during a break from rehearsing her summation. And she was still feeling slightly nauseated, the indigestion no doubt exacerbated by what was happening.

Which still didn't seem real.

"And you think he—"

She choked on the words.

Murder.

Guy.

The two had no business being together in the same sentence.

The functioning part of her mind understood now why they'd sent cops to her house. If they'd called, Guy would have been alerted. Had time to run.

They wanted the element of surprise on their side.

". . . start getting your financials together."

The words broke through the last of her mental haze.

Financials meant money to post bail if Guy wasn't remanded into custody after the first arraignment. Which meant an arrest was imminent. Which meant that the DA believed there was enough evidence for the NYPD to make an arrest based on probable cause.

Enough to take to a grand jury?

"What's your evidence?"

"Come on, Linda. You know better than that."

"And you know better than to try to bluff a bluffer. If you had something, my house would be being searched now, as we speak."

"We have evidence, I can assure you. That's why it's imperative we talk to Guy. Hear his side."

A tactic Linda herself had used when interrogating a suspect. More times than she could count.

It was never about hearing their side. It was about getting them to talk. To confess.

To bury themselves.

"The longer he's AWOL, the worse it will be for him."

AWOL.

In the DA's mind, already tried and convicted.

Her stomach gave another sickening heave.

Diane was still talking. "If he tried to flee the jurisdiction, he won't get far."

Linda thought about that. If Guy had run, where would he go? They didn't own a weekend home. They'd recently finished paying off the mortgage on the Scarsdale house.

Then something occurred to her.

The crime had taken place in the city. That's why NYPD cops showed up at her door.

That meant that Guy never left Manhattan.

His car would be in the lot next to the Scarsdale train station, where he parked it every morning before catching the 8:02.

Which the police were bound to find, if they hadn't found it already.

They'd also be checking all points of entry in and out of the city. Combing every subway, train, and bus station.

Diane was right.

How far could he go without a means of transportation?

"Guy's going to need a good lawyer. You should hire one right away, before the media gets hold of this. We're playing things close to the vest, but you know as well as I do that information can still get out."

Of course it could. And the leaks usually came from the DA's office when it suited their purpose.

"And once they find out who his wife is, things will explode. Better to get in front of this now. As of today, you're officially on leave from the Manhattan District Attorney's office. You can't be anywhere near this case."

19

S he punched in another number on her phone.

"Hey, Linda."

His voice sounded gruffer than usual. In the background, she heard the murmur of a female voice.

"Sorry to get you out of bed."

"It's okay." To someone else, "What?" Static crackled in her ear—his hand over the mouthpiece. "Hold on." Taking the conversation outside. "Sorry."

"I'm the one who should be sorry. I didn't know who else to call."

"You know you can call me twenty-four seven. You of all people."

"Thanks, Pete."

"I'm guessing you talked to Diane."

"For all the good that did."

"Heard anything from Guy?"

Of course he knew. The Manhattan DA's office and the entire NYPD knew by now.

Before she called Pete, she'd tried Guy's cell again. Just as it had when she called earlier, his voicemail message came on immediately, which meant he still had his phone turned off.

Her texts had gone unanswered. Delivered, but not read.

"I haven't heard from him."

She couldn't lie to Pete, even if she wanted to. He always saw right through her.

Peter Randolph had been a private investigator with the DA's office after taking early retirement from the NYPD seven years ago. They'd worked closely together ever since.

"I need to know what they have. Diane wouldn't tell me anything."

She'd never asked anything like this of him, knew it was a conflict of interest. And felt guilty and vaguely ashamed for using their friendship to suss out information.

"You saw the paper?"

"Yes." And wished she hadn't.

It was worse than she'd imagined.

According to the article—the only murder in today's Metro section—and the online story she read immediately afterward that had been trending since the wee hours, the victim's skull had been bashed in with a lamp. Then the victim was strangled with the cord from the same lamp.

The victim's name hadn't been released, but police had already zeroed in on a suspect.

She'd held her breath as she scanned the rest of the article. Nowhere was Guy's name mentioned.

Yet.

"Do you have any idea what Guy was doing there?"

It was the same question she'd been asking herself ever since she read where the body had been found.

In a hotel room downtown on the west side. Not far from Guy's publishing house.

"No."

"Okay. Let me see what I can find out. Give me a couple of hours."

She didn't didn't tell him she was afraid they didn't have that long.

Moments after she put down her phone, the doorbell rang. Dread dogged her steps as she walked to the window and peeked through the curtains.

A blonde in a red suit and a man with a camera slung over his shoulder stood on the doorstep. Two white media vans were parked across the street.

So much for Diane's warning that things would soon explode.

They already had.

20

P ete called back two hours later.

"That was fast."

She'd spent most of the past 120 minutes that dragged on like a prison sentence in bed. Even with her head under the blanket, she kept hearing the shrill sound of the doorbell chiming over and over again in a cruel replay of earlier that morning.

Twenty minutes ago, a bout of intense nausea finally forced her out of bed. She barely made it to the bathroom in time to throw up what remained of last night's dinner.

Or thought she had.

When her cell buzzed, the monster in her belly roared back to life.

"Linda?"

"I'm here." She closed her eyes, willed her stomach to calm down.

"You all right? Sorry. Stupid question."

"No. It's fine." Which of course it wasn't and would likely never be again. She took deep breaths, even though a part of her dreaded what she might hear. But if there was one thing she hated, it was being kept in the dark.

Linda didn't need a psychiatrist to tell her that it stemmed from childhood. From living with an unsolved crime. It was the reason she went into law in the first place, even toyed with law enforcement. But she didn't have the stomach for it.

Instead, she spent her career seeking the justice she hadn't been able to get for her brother, killed by a drunk driver who fled the scene, and whose mangled body lying in the middle of a quiet country lane would haunt her the rest of her life.

She opened her eyes, forced herself to focus. "What have you got?"

"They found something."

"What?"

"Guy's phone."

"Where?" That explained why he hadn't answered her texts and her calls had gone straight to voicemail.

"In the hotel room. Must have fallen out of his pocket."

"Or it was in the room because someone stole it."

It was the lie every defendant told in a futile attempt to prove that they couldn't have commited the crime because they were never there.

"They're checking his call log. They also have physical evidence. Fingerprints."

Her stomach lurched again. "Don't tell me they're on the murder weapon."

"No prints on the lamp or the lamp cord."

Which a prosecutor could argue at trial—and she had, dozens of times—was because the killer wiped off the lamp and lamp cord before fleeing the scene.

"Where were the prints found?"

"One set on the outside of the door. A second set on the inside doorknob. The good news is that the prints are only partials. And we both know how fallible latent evidence is, even with algorithms and image enhancement software. Almost impossible to get a one-hundred-percent match. But they have enough to know that the prints on both surfaces belong to the same person."

"Not the vic?"

"No."

Which meant that the victim didn't let in his killer.

Or get up and walk out of the room after he died.

"There was also an anonymous call to nine-one-one. Someone who heard something. The police figure the killer had to get out of there fast. That's how his prints would have ended up on the inside doorknob. CSU found another set of prints on the card key that was on the bureau. Those were a match to the vic. Which makes sense because he's the one who booked the room. The police think the killer followed the vic into the room. That's why they found prints on the outside of the door."

"Why would he do that?"

"To confront him. They think the killer and the vic were fighting over a woman. They've got a witness. Someone walking his dog thought he saw a woman outside the hotel earlier. They've also got a bartender in the bar around the corner who said Guy had a couple of whiskey shots there. Was drunk and assaulted another patron. Guy was asked to leave."

It just got worse and worse. And Guy was drinking again. "Did they get a description of the woman?"

"The witness was too far away. But he was pretty sure she was a brunette."

That narrowed things down. "Where is she now?"

"No one knows. Apparently there was a couple hundred in cash on the bureau. It was still there when the police arrived."

Cash up front meant a business transaction. "A hooker?"

"That's the likely scenario. The motel clerk said the guests are mostly hookers and their Johns. Heavy concentration of prostitutes in that area."

"What hooker leaves cash on the table?"

"If two Johns start getting violent and she wants to get the hell out of there."

So that was how the NYPD was spinning it.

"She could have grabbed the cash on her way out."

"Maybe she was afraid. From what I hear, the murder was pretty brutal. Place was a wreck. Vic lost a lot of blood. Why are you so hung up on the woman?"

Why was she?

Because she didn't want to believe that Guy was cheating.

But a prostitute? It didn't make sense.

"Who's the vic?"

"Driver's they found in his wallet says he's Stuart Robbins."

The name meant nothing to her.

"Apparently he wasn't a regular at the hotel."

"Is that unusual?"

"Clerk said most of the rooms were booked by returning guests, but he always got a few first-timers."

That raised a red flag. Prosecutors were constantly on the lookout for patterns. Exceptions to the rule stuck out like sore thumbs.

It seemed too convenient.

And now the woman in the middle of it all had vanished.

Then she thought about what he'd told her about the neighborhood being a known hotbed for prostitution.

Was it possible?

Linda couldn't believe she was even thinking about it.

"Pete, do you remember the Claude Colmann case?"

"The predicate felon who was convicted of rape and murder? That was almost six months ago. And you're bringing this up why?"

"You were in the courtroom that day. Remember what happened after the jury came back?"

In less than seven hours, which had set some kind of record at Manhattan Supreme.

After the verdict was read, Colmann's wife ran up to the well to stop the bailiffs as they were leading her husband away. Then she turned her wrath on Linda, screaming that she'd make her pay. She had to be forcibly removed from the courtroom.

The incident haunted Linda. She wasn't sure if it was all that rage directed at her or Frida Colmann's steadfast refusal to believe that her husband could be a monster. A woman so deep in denial she no longer saw reality.

"You saying this is some kind of payback?"

"Could be."

Maybe this wasn't about Guy at all.

Her husband was merely a pawn in a vengeful woman's murderous scheme.

"So according to your scenario, Frida Colmann lured Guy to that hotel room?"

"Why is that so hard to believe? Colmann's an attractive woman." Some of the male jurors had seemed to think so too. "She could have stolen his phone. Planted it in the room."

Pete was quiet for a few minutes. "Let's say, for argument's sake, that Colmann wants to set up Guy for murder. She'd need a victim."

"Right."

"Why Stuart Robbins?"

"How much do we know about him? Maybe he and Colmann knew each other. Maybe she wanted to get back at Robbins for something too. Just because he'd never been in that particular hotel doesn't mean he didn't frequent others. Which could be where his path crossed with Colmann."

"So what happens? Colmann kills Robbins with Guy in the room? And Guy does nothing to try to stop her?"

"The bartender claims Guy had a few shots. Maybe he passed out. Or"—a chill went through her—"Robbins was already dead when Guy got there."

Was Frida Colmann capable of something that diabolical?

"You're talking murder, Linda. A brutal act of violence committed by someone whose only two arrests were for a DWI and solicitation. And there's something else. How could Colmann be sure Guy would take the bait?"

"Isn't it obvious? She seduced him."

"How does something like that happen?"

"What do you mean?"

"It usually takes two."

"I know what you're thinking. My husband's cheating on me, and I'm just making excuses for him. Or maybe what you really mean is he's not just an adulterer, he's a murderer."

"Don't put words in my mouth."

"Tell me that's not what you believe."

"I'm just trying to look out for you. Like always."

"How? By casting aspersions on Guy. He's a good man. He didn't do this." She flopped back down on the bed, her anger spent. "You think I'm grasping at straws, don't you?"

"Honest answer? I really don't know. But I'll check it out, I promise. If there's a connection to Colmann, I'll find it. And Linda?"

"Yes?"

"Take care of yourself."

His voice had dropped, the words delivered in a soft, gentle tone that brought sudden tears to her eyes.

She found herself choking back a sob as he said, "I'll call as soon as I have something."

21

Almost eleven and still no word from Pete.

Or Diane.

That was the call Linda dreaded. Finding out they had Guy in custody.

Even if forensics was able to get something off the partial sets of prints on the outside of the hotel room door and the inside doorknob, they couldn't match the prints to Guy because they wouldn't be in the system.

He'd never been arrested.

They needed him. And knew that he couldn't stay off the radar forever.

It was only a matter of time.

She'd spent the past few hours trying to figure out where he might have gone.

Something the police also wanted to know. Which was why an unmarked car was sitting at the end of the block. They were waiting for Guy to make contact and hoping that Linda would be stupid or desperate enough to lead them to him.

The truth was, she had no idea where Guy was or who he might turn to for help. They didn't have a lot of friends. Just a few couples, mostly professionals from her work life that they had dinner with on occasion.

As for family, Guy was an only child, and she'd been one ever since her brother died.

They had no children.

Not for lack of trying, but she'd been unable to conceive. Guy refused to adopt, which turned into a major issue their marriage almost didn't survive.

All they had was each other.

She'd always felt that it was the two of them against the world. United in their commonality because of the tragedies they'd both endured.

The only thing she could do now was pray that Guy came to his senses and returned home so they could face this together.

But the longer he remained off the radar, the less and less likely it seemed that his actions were those of an innocent man.

So here she sat, hunched over her laptop at the kitchen table, stalking the Internet every few minutes for updates.

Although she'd been expecting it, seeing her husband's name on the screen had been a one-two punch to her far-from-reliable stomach. Making what still felt like a nightmare all too painfully real.

Especially after the detectives who'd come earlier showed up with a search warrant, something she'd known was coming.

She'd trailed them from room to room, feeling outraged and violated. Understanding now how the wives of suspects felt as she watched the two detectives leave with garbage bags filled with Guy's personal items, including his computer.

It was a media circus out there. In the last half hour, the radio and television vans had doubled in number. One was parked directly outside her house. Through the curtain, she saw people she'd known for years standing on their manicured front lawns casting surreptitious glances at her house.

She could just imagine what they were thinking. Could almost hear the whispers.

A murderer living in their peaceful, suburban town.

Which only goes to show that you never know who your neighbors are.

The wife had to be complicit.

And Linda Haley wasn't your average wife. She was a prosecutor who knew the ins and outs of the law and how to bend it for her own ends. She would know all the tricks to help her husband escape justice.

As if Guy were some hardened criminal.

A wave of nausea rolled over her. Linda pushed back from the table and walked on rubbery legs to the cabinet. She pulled out a box of crackers, the only food she could keep down. Followed the crackers with a tall glass of water, and listened to the grandfather clock in the hall tolling the hour.

She couldn't stop thinking about the woman.

Was it Frida Colmann?

Colmann and Guy came from different worlds.

How would they have met?

It would have to have been during those nights she worked late. Guy had started drinking again—a part of her was still angry that he'd broken his promise—so it was logical that he'd go to a bar. Probably went there after work, the way he did the night of the murder.

Colmann would have known where his office was. Studied his schedule. Made their initial encounter look like happenstance.

She might have sat down next to him at a bar. Struck up a conversation. Slowly reeled him in. How difficult would that be?

Guy was fifty-six, a dangerous age. In a professional rut for years, stuck in a dead-end job.

And summer was almost upon them. They were only eight weeks out from the fortieth anniversary of his mother's death.

It was the perfect storm.

Or was she simply making excuses for him?

It usually takes two.

Pete's words when she brought up the possibility of a vendetta orchestrated by Frida Colmann.

To obscure a truth she didn't want to face?

The wife always the last to know?

Guy had seemed distracted lately.

And she was sure now that it was guilt she saw in his eyes.

Those dreamy brown eyes she'd fallen so hard for that rainy spring day twenty-nine years ago. Both going for a cab at the same time. He on his way to a book party, she to a restaurant for a blind date. She never did meet the man, and he never made it to the party.

And now her husband stood accused of a heinous crime.

Being unfaithful was one thing. Adultery wasn't even a crime. Not that that excused the ultimate marital betrayal.

But murder?

Guy lived most of his life with his head in a book, an escape from the brutality of the real world that she'd always secretly envied.

He didn't have a violent bone in his body.

Except when he had a few drinks in him.

No. It wasn't possible.

Guy didn't do this.

When Pete finally called back, at a little before two, the unmarked sedan had moved to the other side of the street.

"Tell me you found a connection to Frida Colmann," Linda said when she picked up.

"No. Sorry."

"What?" She could always tell when he was holding back.

"You're not going to like it."

"Pete—"

"It's about Guy."

22

That night, a sharp cramp roused Linda out of a restless sleep.

In the bathroom, a tampon sat on the porcelain sink. But there was no blood. Not even a trickle. She'd been late only once in all these years, when she was fourteen.

The year Mikey was killed in that hit-and-run. The bicycle he'd been riding was still in her parents' attic.

After bolting out of bed at five-thirty Sunday morning, Linda still felt sick afterward. Even after heaving up half her insides.

She didn't need a pregnancy test to confirm what she'd been suspecting for days.

Life had begun growing in her forty-six-year-old womb.

Against all the odds.

23

"Y ou don't look so good."

"Something I ate. I'll be fine."

Pete didn't believe her. But no way was she telling him the truth. Her husband should be the first to know, the way Linda had always imagined. Even if she'd been the last to know about him.

She still couldn't believe Guy had a record and hadn't told her. Turned out, there were a lot of things he hadn't shared.

"What I don't understand is, if Guy was arrested before, why didn't law enforcement get a hit on his prints?"

The first thing they did was check for priors. And invariably found them. Because ninety-nine percent of the defendants her office prosecuted had committed crimes before.

"Nothing came up on AFIS," Pete said.

"How is that possible?"

"We're talking forty years ago, Linda. Decades before the fingerprint system went digital. Just errors waiting to happen. The ink smudges or fades. Card gets filed wrong. And that's just New York City. In a place like Manatawkett, forget it."

The town where the crime had occurred.

She already knew that, along with the month and year—August 1984—thanks to Pete's inside source.

She was still having trouble processing this. When Pete told her yesterday, she was stunned. A part of her refused to believe him, still hoping it was a vendetta orchestrated by Frida Colmann.

Now she didn't know what to think.

"You sure you're up for this? We can still turn around. I can talk to him, report back to you. Maybe it would be better that way. Cop to cop."

Pete had also found out the name of the detective who handled the 1984 homicide case.

That was the crime in the sealed record.

Murder.

Linda could swear her heart almost stopped when Pete told her that. The only bright spot was that the Manatawkett DA had dismissed the charges against Guy. Pete ferreted out that detail as well.

He'd already gone above and beyond, risking his job by feeding her information no one had access to without a court order.

Linda looked at him now. At his big, strong hands gripping the steering wheel.

They'd been on the road over an hour, leaving very early this morning in a car Pete had rented rather than her car, which would be easier to spot. She snuck out the back door to avoid the media and elude the police.

It was already after eight.

For so early on a Sunday morning, the Long Island Expressway was surprisingly busy. But they were only a week out from July, the height of the summer season.

"I have to go, Pete," Linda said. "I need to know what happened out there."

And find out what? That her husband was a two-time killer?

She refused to believe that.

Refused to allow herself to believe that.

The only thing in her favor was that her boss didn't know she knew about the sealed record. But it was only a matter of time before the Manhattan DA made the motion to unseal.

Then Manatawkett would be crawling with NYPD.

She needed to get answers before that happened. Before Diane found out that Linda was here after being put on official leave and ordered to stay away from the case.

The current case.

Her boss didn't say anything about the '84 case.

Pete took swig from his water bottle as he moved into the faster-moving left lane. "Guy never talked to you about that summer?"

Linda forced her mind away from the fact that she was also risking her own career. "Not much. All I know is that it was the last vacation he and his parents took as a family. A few weeks after they came back to the city, his mother killed herself."

"You never told me how she died."

"Rachel Kingship slit her wrists with her husband's straight razor. When the police came, Guy was sitting on the floor of his parents' bedroom with his mother's body in his lap. He was covered in her blood."

"Jesus."

"Guy was the one who found her. But he has no actual memory of that night. He only knows what he was told. His doctors at the time said the trauma was too great for his mind to accept. The summer vacation in Manatawkett had been his mother's last gift to him. Guy graduated from high school a year early because of his high academic scores. He was supposed to start college in the fall. He didn't end up going until two years later."

Linda sipped from her can of soda, the carbonation helping to calm her stomach. "All these years, I thought he didn't talk about that summer because of his mother's suicide at the end of August."

Pete shook his head. "How do you ever come back from something like that?"

"I don't think you do. Guy's way of coping was to put the past in a box."

She'd never been able to master that particular skill.

Maybe it was a guy thing.

Or a Guy thing.

"What about his father?"

"Louis Kingship was a piece of work. A Manhattan Supreme Court judge who was also a drunk. An abuser who turned his fists on his wife and son. Apparently, it wasn't a secret. There were rumors that sexual abuse had gone on at the courthouse. But the victims were afraid to come forward."

Especially in the early eighties; decades before the Me Too movement.

"A few months after Rachel Kingship committed suicide, Kingship was asked to step down from the bench. He died of cirrhosis of the liver a year later."

Guy had hated his father. His greatest fear was that he'd turn into the man who'd terrorized his mother and him throughout his boyhood.

That was why Linda insisted he stop drinking.

"You think the abuse was the reason for his mother's suicide?"

"Probably, but who can ever really know what's in a person's head?" Always in the back of her mind was the fear that Guy would actually follow in Rachel Kingship's footsteps.

Their exit was coming up on the right.

Pete turned off the highway and onto a side road, where they stopped at a gas station to refuel and pick up some snacks.

As they pulled out of the station for the last leg of the journey, Linda couldn't stop her mind from retreating to the dark place. Where memories of her dead brother lived.

Now she was afraid that Guy was gone too.

Lost to her forever.

24

She must have dozed off.

When Linda opened her eyes, there was a long line of cars in front of them.

The two lanes were merging into one.

Route 27 was the only way in and out of the towns and villages at the eastern end of Long Island.

The same road Guy had traveled with his parents all those years ago.

PART II

25

1984

G uy stared out the window, trying to ignore the tension in the car. He was barely aware of the passing scenery. Not that there was much to see on this sprawling, seemingly endless four-lane highway.

Everything felt worse now, in the cramped confines of the sedan his father drove, too cheap to spring for a new car. Guy felt trapped in this clunky piece of machinery where you felt every bump on the road.

What he secretly fantasized about was having one of those cool sports cars that half the kids in his class had gotten as high school graduation presents.

His present—something his mother fought for and, unusual for her, won—was spending the summer in Manatawkett.

Guy had never been there, but he adored the beach. He used to love summer weekends at the shore with his mother when he was a kid, when the two of them would drive out to the bungalow they'd rented in the Far Rockaways in Queens and spend the day reading together on the sand.

Before his father arrived on the Friday night train from the city.

Before Louis Kingship became looser with his fists.

In the passenger seat, his mother must have sensed his thoughts, because she turned around. Her brown eyes—a mirror image of his—were filled with love. Her mouth was turned up in a reassuring smile he'd seen so many times before.

Guy didn't feel reassured.

And the trip was starting to drag on.

He watched his father's hands clench around the steering wheel as if his fingers were itching to hold a shot glass. And Guy knew what that meant. He got a sinking sensation in the pit of his stomach. This whole family togetherness vacation was feeling more and more like a mistake.

And he'd rather have gotten a Triumph for graduation.

Though he'd die before he let his mother know.

He must have fallen asleep. When Guy opened his eyes, his left cheek was smashed against the window.

Up ahead, the two lanes they'd been driving on had become one. The vegetation on the right side of the highway was thinning out.

He could hear the surf before he had his first glimpse of the ocean. When the deep, deep blue of the sea finally came into view, he was struck, as always, by the sight of those magnificent whitecaps rising into the sky.

He could still hear the waves crashing against the shore long after the highway had widened into a seemingly endless stretch of road. The ocean was once again hidden behind tall dunes.

They drove past a sandy lot filled with cars and families acting as if they were having a great time at tables shaded by white-and-yellow umbrellas next to a red sign proclaiming CLAM BAR in white letters. Nearby was a wooden placard asking customers PLEASE WAIT HERE TO BE SEATED.

Now they were coming to a fork in the road that veered off to a narrow, winding road toward what looked like an older part of the town.

The road started to rise as they continued due east, then abruptly sloped down as they approached the center of town. The sight of a low, squat white building with a gray roof and a lamppost out front called the Memory Motel made Guy smile. The name struck a chord; started him thinking that it would make a great title for the book he dreamed about someday writing.

In the rearview mirror, his father was watching him, his face darkened by his usual angry scowl. You never knew what was going to set him off. His mother always walked on eggshells around him.

Not that it ever did any good.

Things only got worse after the day Louis Kingship came home and found Guy and his mother trying to leave. Something that his father would never let them forget.

Guy's head started to pound in rhythm with the roar of the surf, the sea once again visible as the road curved.

He barely noticed passing the Manatawkett town limits.

Seeing a drive-in, followed by a miniature golf course.

A deli, with a green-and-white awning.

An oyster shack.

A hardware store.

A diner.

A tackle shop, where Guy could see fishermen on benches mending nets.

When they finally pulled up to a gray, two-story house with an American flag out front where his parents had rented two rooms, Guy's earlier euphoria was gone.

All he wanted to do was escape from the car, run across the sand, and pretend that he was just a normal kid without a care in the world.

26

I t was shaping up to be a beautiful day. The sun was warm, the sky an expanse of uninterrupted blue.

Linda rolled down the passenger window to breathe in the fresh sea air. The ocean was hugging the shore on their right, and she could see a smattering of early morning beachgoers digging umbrellas into the sand, as if staking out their personal territory.

Had Guy spent time at the beach that summer? Reading the classics he loved on a towel on the sand? Swimming in the ocean? Riding the waves?

She still felt a sense of betrayal that he'd kept Manatawkett a secret from her. It made her wonder what else he hadn't shared with her.

With every mile that brought her closer to the place her husband had spent that long-ago summer, it felt as he were moving farther and farther away. The man she'd lived with for almost thirty years becoming a stranger.

Linda had never felt so powerless.

She was used to dealing in facts. Facts were immutable. Unassailable. Facts won her convictions.

Now she was afraid of them. Afraid of what the facts in the '84 case would turn out to be.

"You okay?"

She started to nod, then shook her head.

Pete reached out and covered her hand with his.

The warmth of his touch spread through her body, calming and soothing her as they drove.

Seeing her hand grasped in his bigger one comforted her in a way that she hadn't felt in a long time.

27

"**H**ungry?"

Linda and Pete were sitting on a bench on Main Street, which was already crowded with vacationers taking leisurely strolls and peering in shop windows on this late June Sunday morning.

The seventh day was the one day when Chief of Police Mike Bonaker rested, according to the desk sergeant Linda and Pete had spoken with at the Manatawkett precinct.

Bonaker always attended the ten a.m. service at the Manatawkett Community Church, which was followed by a brunch given on the last Sunday of every month. After that, the police chief could often be found with his rod and tackle in his dinghy on Manatawkett Harbor pursuing his favorite pastime.

It was twenty-five past ten.

"Linda? I know it's early, but you look like you could use a little sustenance."

Pete was pointing at a building with a green awning halfway down the block that looked as if it had been there forever.

All she'd managed to keep down that morning was tea and a few saltine crackers. Just the thought of food made her queasy, but Linda knew she had to eat, especially now that she was fairly certain she was pregnant.

She nodded. "Okay."

An old-fashioned bell above the deli's front door tinkled as Linda and Pete walked in. The booths and stand-alone tables were occupied, but they found two seats at the counter.

Their orders were taken by a grizzled, white-haired man with an apron covering his overalls. Like the deli itself, with its retro decor, he looked like a throwback to an earlier era.

"Haven't seen you folks before," he said as he poured coffee for Pete. "You here for the summer?"

"Just visiting," Pete said.

"Tourists, huh? Summer's when we get most of them. And of course the weekend city folks. They all pretty much clear out after Labor Day. We even have a name for it: Tumbleweed Tuesday. That's when we take back our town."

"Actually, we're looking for information about a murder that took place here in 1984." Linda wanted to head him off before he could go off on a tangent about what was clearly a pet peeve about the summer residents versus the locals.

The old-timer nodded as he set down a mug with steaming water and a wedge of lemon in front of Linda. He didn't seem surprised by the question. "Whole thing was dead and buried for decades. No one ever thought she'd come back. Reporters swarmed the town for weeks after she killed herself. Two days after Christmas. I read the highest rate of suicides is over the holidays."

"Who died?" Pete asked.

"You don't know? I figured that was why you were here asking about the old case. Name was Dorothy Miller. She left town in '84. Never heard another word about her until she came back last December and took a header off the roof of the abandoned lighthouse. Wasn't the first suicide up there either. Back in the early nineteen hundreds, the original lighthouse keeper hanged himself from a rope in the observation tower."

He shook his head.

"Shame of it is, local groups have been lobbying to tear down the lighthouse for decades. Lots of folks believe it's haunted, especially now with three people dead. The place really is a death trap, with her loose mortar joints and crumbling railings. Miracle she's still standing, or maybe that's her curse. Thought this latest tragedy might finally light a fire under the town's feet. All it did was dredge up the old murder."

"You talking about what happened in '84?" Pete asked.

"Uh-huh."

"Who was the murder victim?" Linda asked.

"Alfred Johnson. Another local kid. Also took a header off the lighthouse roof. Murder was never solved. Even with Miller's death, I don't know if it ever will be. Reporters stopped coming around after a while. Whole thing'll probably get buried again. Excuse me."

The old-timer stepped away to give checks to several diners. When he returned, he was shaking his head. "Wish I could tell you more. The beach was really packed that night. Bonfire always drew big crowds."

"There was a bonfire the night of the murder?" Pete asked.

The old-timer nodded. "Town holds one every August. Beach was packed. It's a wonder anyone saw or heard anything. The police station was buzzing, though. Happens every year. Kids get drunk. Start fights. Drive under the influence. Couple of arrests. But nothing like what happened at the lighthouse."

"So someone reported something?" Linda asked. Witness statements taken by the police would be in the sealed record.

"Don't know about that. Reporters wanted answers too. But you're talking forty years ago." The old-timer squinted at Linda from beneath bushy white brows. "You writing a story? Would be nice to set the record straight once and for all."

"What do you mean?"

A *ding* sounded from the kitchen. "Hold on." He stepped away again before coming back with two plates he set down in front of Linda and Pete.

In the last few minutes, the place had emptied out. The old-timer leaned against the counter, ready to settle in for a chat. Or the chance to talk about the crime that he obviously saw as a blight on his town.

"What happened in '84 divided Manatawkett." He lowered his voice even though Linda and Pete were the only ones left at the counter. "Some folks thought a girl was at the lighthouse that night, having sex with a couple of boys. Others believed a girl was assaulted there. There were stories about kids who might have seen or heard something. That fired up the rumors that an assault did take place. Miller's name started making the rounds. And Alfred Johnson was killed because he was in the wrong place at the wrong time."

"What was the police's theory?" Pete asked.

"Mike Bonaker was in charge back then. Took the whole thing hard. He was sure Miller had been assaulted. Her suicide confirmed it for him."

And he would be right.

Thoughts of suicide were common among the rape victims whose cases Linda had prosecuted, though not all of them acted on it. Especially four decades later.

But some scars never healed.

"Trouble was, back then there were all these conflicting stories. Miller ended up leaving town. Bonaker couldn't nail anyone for an attack no one could be sure really happened. But someone was arrested for Johnson's murder. Name was never in the paper. Rumors were he was a kid from the city."

Linda closed her eyes.

"What was the evidence against him?" Pete asked.

"He was on the lighthouse roof that night. Some kids who'd left the bonfire and were walking down the beach saw someone go off the roof. Called the police from their car phone. When Mike Bonaker went up to the roof, he found the boy. Nobody else."

"What about the possible assault? Did the police have any suspects?"

"There was all sorts of gossip about a bunch of city kids tooling around town in their fancy convertibles. But nothing came of it. When the charges against the boy were dropped, it pissed off a lot of people. 'Til my dying day, I'll never forget standing on the beach and watching Johnson's body fished out of the ocean. Whole town turned out for his funeral. He was a good kid. Didn't deserve what happened to him."

There it was again. The thinly veiled hostility against the interlopers in his town.

Linda set down the grilled cheese she'd barely eaten. Whatever appetite she'd had gone the moment she heard Guy had been on the lighthouse roof.

"There is someone you might want to talk to. Hank Bistrian claims he saw Miller on the beach that night. But I've got to warn you. He's in his nineties. Not always compos mentis, if you know what I mean."

"Know where we can find him?" Pete asked.

The old man nodded. "Where he usually is most days, even Sunday. Sitting on a bench behind the tackle shop."

28

Hank Bistrian was exactly where the old-timer at the deli said he'd be. On a bench outside the tackle shop.

He was wearing faded denim jeans and a white white knit jersey with "Manatawkett" written across it in bold blue letters. He appeared to be asleep.

Until Linda and Pete approached, and his eyes snapped open.

"Looking for someone?" His voice was deep and rough with age, but there was barely a wrinkle on his tanned face.

"You," Pete said. "Your friend at the deli told us we'd find you here."

"And here I am."

"You're Hank Bistrian?"

"Who wants to know?"

"I'm Pete and this is Linda."

Bistrian nodded but didn't take Pete's outstretched hand. "Now you going to tell me why you're here?"

"We wanted to talk about what happened in August of '84. We were told you saw Dorothy Miller the night Alfred Johnson was killed."

Bistrian's blue eyes narrowed. "You cops?"

Despite his advanced age, little seemed to slip by him.

"We're writing about what happened here," Linda said. They'd decided during the short drive over to stick to that story. "We heard not everyone was agreed on what took place on the roof of the abandoned lighthouse."

"You can say that again." Bistrian's voice turned bitter. "Mike Bonaker kept trying to get me to change my story. Say I didn't see what I saw."

"What did you see?"

Bistrian didn't answer. His head suddenly lolled on his neck, and his eyes fluttered closed. When he opened his eyes, he stared at them as if he'd never seen them before.

"Can I help you folks?"

The old-timer had warned them, but it was still unsettling to witness. Where Bistrian's eyes had been sharp and searching a few moments earlier, they were now rheumy and unfocused.

He didn't seem to expect an answer. "I was dreaming about my wife. Then I remembered she was dead. Terrible thing, outliving your spouse."

"Mr. Bistrian—"

"How do you know my name?"

Pete sat down next to him. "Your friend at the deli."

"Jed Whalen? Who told you we were friends?"

Linda ignored the question. "Mr. Whalen thought you could tell us about what you saw on the beach the night Alfred Johnson died."

Bistrian nodded. "I saw her. I don't care what anyone says."

"You saw Dorothy Miller?"

Bistrian nodded again, more vehemently this time, his eyes once again clear.

"What was she doing?"

"Walking down the beach. Fast, like she was in a hurry. Like she was meeting someone. Then I remembered how she acted when I saw her earlier."

"Where?" Linda asked.

"She came into my store that afternoon. I owned the general store back then. Sold it to a chain in oh-five. Worst decision I ever made. Those damn stores not only destroyed the beauty and peace of towns like ours, they took away people's livelihoods."

"What time did Dorothy Miller come into your store?" Linda asked, heading him off before he could continue his lament against Manatawkett's gentrification. Out of step with something that had been going on for years.

"Funny, I can't remember where I left my reading glasses this morning. But I remember that afternoon like it happened yesterday. It was around two o'clock. I'd just finished my lunch. She'd been in my store before, but this time was different. She seemed excited. Like maybe she had a hot date that night after her shift at the yacht club."

"The Manatawkett Yacht Club?" Linda recalled passing the place earlier as they drove into town.

Bistrian nodded. "She waited tables there. Been doing that since high school. They kept her on after she graduated. Anyways, it struck me that day because in all the years I knew her, I never saw her with a man. Figured it was because of her stepfather."

"Who was he?" Pete asked.

"You haven't heard about Lucas Trask? There were rumors about Miller and her stepfather. The things folks love to gossip about. And Miller's mother turned a blind eye. That kind of sensational stuff. Trask left town a few weeks after Dorothy Miller did. Her mother died about ten years ago. Miller didn't come back for the funeral."

"Did people really believe Dorothy Miller was having a relationship with her stepfather?" Linda asked.

Bistrian shrugged. "Who's to say? Folks make up stories and they're taken as gospel."

He was right. Although she'd long ago convinced herself that she was pursuing a noble mission, Linda knew that trials were rarely about finding the truth.

It was about which side told the best story for the jury to believe.

"Did you have any idea who Miller might have been meeting?" Pete asked.

Bistrian shook his head. "But she bought a lipstick and some perfume, and she was smiling like she had a secret. When I saw her hurrying down the beach that night, I figured I was right."

"Where was she headed?"

"I couldn't say a hundred percent, but I thought it might have been the old lighthouse. I remember wondering at the time why she'd be going there. Nobody had set foot in that place in years. Guess that was the point. Turned out I was right.'

"Did you actually see Miller go into the lighthouse?" Linda asked.

Bistrian didn't respond. He was staring at a man in a tan windbreaker who'd come out of the tackle shop carrying a fishing rod. Bistrian's gaze followed the man as he walked to his truck.

"God, I miss those days. Spent some of the best hours of my life on Manatawkett Harbor. Caught a few big fish too. Never landed a great white, though."

"Mr. Bistrian?"

"Did you know she went down near here? With four fishermen aboard. All these years later, divers are still out there trying to find her lost hull. Never found the bodies."

Linda tried to tamp down her frustration. "Mr. Bistrian, did you see Dorothy Miller go into the lighthouse the night Alfred Johnson was killed?"

Bistrian frowned, trying to remember. "I got distracted. Refilling coolers. Putting out fresh supplies. It was close to midnight. The beach was packed. Bonfire going full blast. I doubt I would have been able to pick her out after that with so many people coming and going."

"You said Mike Bonaker tried to get you to change your story. Why?" Pete asked.

"Bonaker had his own idea about what happened and wouldn't budge. Said Miller's attackers trapped her inside the lighthouse, leaving her nowhere to run but up to the roof. Some say she was assaulted up there. Others believe it happened down below, in a corner under the stairs."

"Did Bonaker have evidence of any of that?" Linda asked.

"You'd have to ask him. If he did, no one knew what it was. You probably heard Bonaker arrested the kid who was on the roof that night. But he had to let him go."

A pained look crossed his face, either from being forced to relive something distressing or the toll the effort of remembering was taking.

"What do you think happened that night?" Pete asked.

"I think Dorothy Miller met someone at the lighthouse and ended up getting assaulted. And Alfred Johnson was a witness."

Not what Linda wanted to hear.

"Wish I could tell you folks more, but that's all I know. Now I gotta get back to work." He indicated the pile of nets under the bench. "Keeps me busy. Guess that's all you can ask for at my age."

"Thanks for your time," Pete said.

"Sure."

As Linda and Pete started to leave, Bistrian's voice stopped them.

"It's personal, isn't it?"

Linda turned around. Bistrian was looking at her.

"Excuse me?"

"Your interest in what happened." He stretched out his legs as he leaned back against the bench. "Whatever it is, I hope you find what you're looking for."

29

1984

I t was raining.

Big, fat drops that fell from the sky like manna from heaven and lightened Guy's heart.

Rain meant that he couldn't go fishing with his father, Louis Kingship's twisted idea of male bonding. Guy had already done that once since they arrived, sitting in a rowboat on Lake Manatawkett for hours, waiting to feel a tug on the line. Hating the sight of the struggling fish on the hook, fighting for its life. He'd thrown the fish back into the water, which enraged his father and earned him a beating that night.

Rain meant that he couldn't take the tennis lesson Louis Kingship had arranged at the Manatawkett Yacht Club.

Instead, Guy got to spend the whole glorious day at the library.

With his father busy reviewing court papers and his mother lying down, he made his escape. Guy barely felt the rain pelting his umbrella

as he walked to the cottage that sat on the property of the Manatawkett
Community Church.

He'd read up on the library and discovered that it had started life as
a bookmobile relying on donated books before moving into the cottage.

The rain had let up a little by the time Guy arrived at the library.

He shook out his umbrella, closed it, and bounded up to the front
door with the peeling paint that seemed well suited to the literary
authors concealed behind its humble facade. He couldn't wait to get his
hands on the next book in the ambitious schedule he'd set for himself
after graduating high school, to read a classic a week.

◆

The following morning dawned bright and clear.

Figuring his mother was safe while his father slept it off, Guy felt
he could relax his vigilance and slipped out of the house once again.

He was on a towel reading when he saw a girl emerge from the water
like some otherworldly sea nymph.

Guy watched her take off her bathing cap and shake out her long,
auburn hair.

She wore a one-piece swimsuit the color of the sea and had legs that
seemed to go on forever.

She was the most beautiful girl he'd ever seen.

30

1984

O ver the next few days, Guy saw her everywhere.

He saw her across from the tackle shop while he sat on a bench waiting for his father, who was inside buying bait. She was walking down the street peering in shop windows with another girl who was tall and had short, blond hair and broad shoulders.

He saw her passing outside Mr. Jack's Pancake House on Main Street as he sat with his parents at a table by the window wolfing down eggs over easy with waffles and a side of rye toast while his father argued with the waiter about his overcooked bacon.

He saw her in the supermarket one afternoon, where he was shopping with his mother. She was in the produce aisle, selecting a melon. She looked so pretty in dark blue shorts that matched her eyes and a white T-shirt, her auburn hair swept up in a high ponytail.

She didn't notice him.

That same night, he was sitting at a table in the dining room of the Manatawkett Yacht Club, his father complaining how much the meal was going to set him back, when he saw her come out of the kitchen balancing a tray of plates.

He held his breath, praying their table was in her section. A few minutes later, she approached them. When she handed them menus and their fingers brushed, he felt the reaction in every part of his body.

Two mornings later, he was walking on the sand when he saw her dive into the water and vanish beneath a breaking wave.

When she finally emerged and shook her hair from her bathing cap the way he'd seen her do that first morning, he told himself that this time he wasn't going to miss his chance.

He was on his feet and gathering the courage to approach her when she walked toward him. He saw her towel a few feet away and realized that she had to pass his towel to get to hers.

Afterward, Guy wasn't sure who made the first move. But suddenly they were standing next to each other and he was introducing himself.

When they shook hands, hers was still damp from the ocean.

"Dorothy Miller." Her voice was low and lilting, as lovely as the rest of her, with a smile that took his breath away. "Pleased to meet you, Guy Kingship. What are you reading?" She indicated the book in his hand.

It took Guy a moment to gather his wits. Then he showed her the cover of the book he'd taken out of the library. "What do you like to read?"

She shrugged. "I couldn't say, to tell you the truth. I don't have a lot of free time. But I would like to read more. Maybe you can suggest some books. I'll bet you have your favorite authors."

"Sure," Guy said, his mind already whirling with which books to get her started on. "I've been reading since I was a kid."

A silence fell.

"Are you from around here?" he asked.

She nodded, but her smile seemed to slip a little. "Lived in this town my whole life. How about you?"

"This is the first time I've been to Manatawkett."

"Where are you from?"

"New York City."

"Wow. I've never been to New York."

"You should come visit. I'll show you around."

Then they both just stood there, the day breaking around them, the thunder of the surf the perfect backdrop to what was happening between them.

Guy's mouth was dry, his heart raced, and he wondered whether she was feeling the same way.

31

1984

*D*orothy.

Guy loved saying her name. Loved the sound of it; how the three syllables seemed to roll off his tongue.

They spent every free moment together.

Taking early morning walks on the beach.

Sharing lobster rolls at a place that looked like a shack on a stretch of winding road where you could hear the ocean on the other side of the tall dunes.

Sitting together on a blanket on the sand, Guy reading aloud from a book or talking about his favorite authors, Dorothy hanging on his every word.

There never seemed to be enough time.

Guy didn't like leaving his mother alone with his father for too long, so he always made sure to be back at the rental house before eleven, the time Louis Kingship usually arose.

Dorothy had to be home in time to shower and get ready for her waitressing shift at the Manatawkett Yacht Club.

She lived in a house with her best friend, Nancy, the tall, blond girl he had seen her with across the street from the tackle shop.

When he asked about her parents, Dorothy's face changed. All she'd say was that she moved in with Nancy during her senior year of high school.

Guy knew there were things that Dorothy wasn't telling him.

Just as there were things he hadn't shared with her.

Everyone had secrets.

32

They were passing a building that sat on a small rise on the north side of the road, just east of the town.

Linda felt her eyes uncharacteristically fill as she gazed out the passenger window at the imposing, three-story structure with the words MANATAWKETT LIBRARY stenciled in bold black letters on the side.

Guy had always loved libraries.

She was already thinking about him in the past tense, her feeling of betrayal now overridden by worry. She still had no idea where he was.

What she did know was that Guy's SUV hadn't been found at the Scarsdale train station.

Which meant that he'd fled Manhattan and come back for his car.

A risk and an act of premeditation. Of cool, calculated reasoning that was usually attributable to suspects attempting to escape the law.

Guilty suspects.

Linda refused to believe that. Her mantra for the past twenty-four hours.

That's why she was here. Investigating Guy's past.

But she couldn't escape the unsettling feeling that in retracing his steps, she was walking over her husband's grave.

Linda tried to shake off her morbid thoughts. This kind of emotional wallowing wasn't going to help her.

Or Guy.

She and Pete had come to Manatawkett to see Mike Bonaker, who at the moment was unavailable. No guarantee that he'd even talk to them.

There was a good chance that the NYPD or the Manhattan DA's office had already reached out to the Manatawkett cop. They'd want the official version of events from that long-ago night so they could use the old crime to impeach Guy at trial if he testified in his own defense in the current case.

Instead of providing answers, the very different conversations Linda and Pete had had with the two local men only raised more questions.

"We don't know why Guy was on the lighthouse roof that night," Pete said, attuned to her as always. "Or that he committed a crime. The charges were dismissed, which means Bonaker didn't have enough evidence to bring to the Suffolk County DA to get an indictment. Let's not jump to conclusions until we have more information."

That was why they were on their way to the yacht club where Dorothy Miller had been a waitress forty years ago.

The hope being that Miller's suicide in December might have triggered people's memories, even though neither Jed Whalen at the deli nor Hank Bistrian said anything to indicate that anyone had had an epiphany.

Or come forward with new information.

Even reporters had stopped nosing around.

It was a long shot, covering ground that had been gone over six months ago.

Linda was hoping that someone might recall something they hadn't remembered back in '84. Or this past December.

Maybe Miller had had a friend in whom she'd confided. Girls often shared details about their love lives.

Especially if there was someone special in Dorothy Miller's life, as Hank Bistrian seemed to believe.

33

Reverend Havens had just left the podium, and organ music once again filled the church.

Mike Bonaker nodded at his fellow congregants as they passed his row on their way out, the same as he'd been doing every Sunday morning for decades.

Some parishioners were gone now, of course. No longer the faces of the people he grew up with, attending Sunday services back when Manatawkett was a sleepy fishing hamlet he'd sworn to protect on the day he graduated from the police academy.

Forty years ago, as a rookie sergeant, he'd failed to deliver on that promise.

And eleven months ago, when his Ruby was dying, he hadn't been able to keep her safe either. Since then, he'd felt adrift, a man without direction.

He needed something to make him feel alive again. To give him purpose.

Now he was playing a waiting game.

It felt as if he was always waiting.

Waiting for backup.

Waiting for a judge to sign off on a search warrant.

Waiting for a suspect to give up the ghost.

Waiting for the DA to decide whether they had enough evidence to take a case to trial.

Waiting for the call from a lab telling him they were able to lift DNA off of a torn, bloodstained chain after nearly four decades.

The odds were better than fifty-fifty. It depended on the quality of the gold.

Nancy Conklin had just risen from her seat in the pew two rows in front of him. Her head was down as she walked through the chapel, the once-blond hair she'd always worn cut close to her face long gone gray.

She was approaching his row.

Sensing his eyes on her, she looked up, the corners of her mouth lifting slightly. He'd rarely seen her smile in all these years, but there was a darkness in her pale blue eyes and a rigid set to her jaw that hadn't been there six months ago.

Bonaker understood her anger. He'd felt it ever since the whole terrible business was dredged up this past December.

It was 1984 all over again, except that after nearly forty years, many of the witnesses had died, moved away, or simply couldn't remember. Still, he needed to make sense of the rumors that had circulated back then, Dorothy Miller's death confirming his belief that Alfred Johnson was killed in '84 because of what he witnessed.

Tragically, Miller's death gave Bonaker a second chance to set things right.

Conklin was still looking at him as she passed his row, nodding as if they were coconspirators.

Nancy Conklin also wanted things set right.

That was why, back in March, Bonaker's first instinct was to show her the torn chain. He'd hoped that seeing it might jog Conklin's memory.

When Alfred Johnson's body was fished out of the ocean that long-ago night, they found welts and bruises on his neck.

If he'd been wearing a gold chain, it was never found. Bonaker figured the killer had taken it with him. Or thrown it in the ocean, where it sat at the bottom of the sea for decades.

Neither scenario turned out to be the case.

And a few months ago, the torn chain had found its way to him.

Strangulation wasn't the cause of Alfred Johnson's death.

It was Johnson's body hitting the water from a height of more than 111 feet. But physical evidence on the torn chain could go a long way toward identifying his murderer—and the way Bonaker saw it, the rapists who killed Johnson to cover up their crime.

In her '84 statement, Conklin told Bonaker she wasn't sure if Johnson had been wearing the gold chain she'd given him as a high school graduation present that night. She wept as she talked, still in shock and grief over the tragedy that had sent the town reeling.

And Miller's death had reopened old wounds.

But not the '84 cold case. His boss, the current Manatawkett precinct commander, told Bonaker that with recent budget cuts, he couldn't afford to supply manpower without solid evidence.

After all this time, how could he give Nancy Conklin false hope?

So far, he'd struck out at two local labs. Three weeks ago, he brought the chain to a lab in Riverhead that boasted more advanced DNA technologies.

Maybe the third time would be the charm.

He owed it to Alfred Johnson and Dorothy Miller.

And Nancy Conklin.

The town owed it to them.

Bonaker had never been a particularly religious man, even in the worst days of his wife's illness.

But now he closed his eyes and prayed, and made a silent promise.

It was time to make the living answer to the dead.

To get the justice that was forty years coming.

34

1984

As the weeks passed, the beach got more crowded, even early in the morning.

Guy became more and more desperate to find a place where he and Dorothy could be alone.

A couple of times, they ended up in the back seat of his parents' car. It was an unnerving experience, Dorothy getting uptight when Guy locked the doors. He had to open all the windows. She told him later that she had a problem being in closed-in spaces.

They'd kiss for a while. Then, like clockwork, she'd change. Her breathing becoming more labored. Shrinking away from him as he caressed her, her beautiful blue eyes filled with fear. Shaking in his arms as he tried to calm her down—wondering who'd made her so afraid—swearing he'd never hurt her. Feeling cheap and diminished in the back seat of his father's sedan, glad that she wasn't ready to go all the way.

Wanting their first time to be special.

35

1984

Guy found the perfect place one mid-July afternoon while walking on the beach with his mother.

Sitting on a high bluff overlooking the ocean was the stuff of Manatawkett legend, an abandoned lighthouse haunted by the spirit of the original lighthouse keeper, who'd been found hanging from a rope in the observation tower on the roof.

Nobody had died there since.

At the library, Guy discovered that the 111-foot structure, once a beacon for ships, had long been closed to visitors. There'd been talk of tearing it down for years.

Not only did this appeal to his sense of history, but when Guy visited the long-defunct lighthouse, he felt an instant connnection.

Granted, she was crumbling in places, the exposed brick of her walls covered in grime. The ground was rough and uneven, and her badly weathered exterior needed a lot more than a fresh coat of paint.

Guy could hear the seagulls screaming through the small, circular windows he passed as he climbed the three sets of spiral iron stairs. Seeing the shadow of their wings as they flew past; blotting out the sky as they ascended with him.

He was out of breath by the time he'd climbed the 137 steps to the top. But when he walked out onto the roof, not even the sight of the decayed, century-old observation tower in the center where the lighthouse keeper had taken his life could dim his excitement. Especially when he looked down and saw the magnificent whitecaps as they rose up to meet the sky.

He'd never felt so free.

Dorothy didn't share his feelings. She got spooked when Guy took her there. She'd grown up with the tall tales, and while she didn't believe them, the shadowy dimness inside the lighthouse frightened her.

Especially the dark corner under the stairs.

But when Guy led her up to the roof and they stood together near the railing, Dorothy was awestruck at the view.

That was when Guy started sneaking out of the rental house after his parents were asleep and Dorothy had finished her three-to-eleven shift at the yacht club.

Gradually, Dorothy started to relax. On the lighthouse roof, there were no car doors hemming them in. Nothing for her to be afraid of up here, surrounded by stars and sea and open space.

It was the most romantic setting Guy could imagine, with the moon shining down from above and the ocean churning far below.

The perfect place to be alone with the girl he loved.

36

When Linda and Pete pulled up to the valet station of the Manatawkett Yacht Club, a gangly kid with sandy hair and the club logo on his white polo shirt walked over to their car.

Outside her window, Linda saw a set of brown-shingled buildings with sloping rooflines that fronted the ocean. As Pete handed the keys to the valet, the sound of the sea seemed to grow louder until it became an incessant drumbeat in her head, drowning out everything else.

If only it could drown out her thoughts.

By the time she and Pete left the yacht club a little over an hour later, they had a name.

Alan Reckson, whose family had owned the Manatawkett Yacht Club for two generations, was too young to remember Dorothy Miller. But he was working there in December when she plunged to her death from the lighthouse roof.

Reckson's parents had retired to Florida several years earlier, and his father remembered Miller. He thought she'd moved in with a girlfriend at one point, but he couldn't recall the friend's name. He thought she might have worked at the yacht club too.

Reckson told Linda and Pete that he said the same thing to reporters who came sniffing around after Miller's death.

He couldn't provide any additional information. And the current thirty-something waitstaff certainly couldn't. But Reckson did give Linda and Pete the name of a man who'd worked at the yacht club for forty-five years, graduating from busboy to waiter to assistant cook and, eventually, to head chef.

Until he was forced to retire a year ago, after being diagnosed with lung cancer.

37

T he petite woman who answered the door wearing a gray dress and a strand of pearls around her thin neck did not look pleased to see them. This was despite the fact that Linda had called ahead, having easily found the phone number and address when she Googled the Manatawkett white pages.

"You can't stay long," Faith Edwards said by way of greeting. "Doctors don't want a lot of visitors."

"We only need a few minutes," Linda said.

Edwards grudgingly opened the door wider to allow them access. As Linda and Pete stepped into a dimly lit hallway, she asked, "You said you were visiting from New York? What did you want to talk to my husband about?"

"Dorothy Miller. We heard he knew her when she worked at the yacht club."

"It never ends, does it?"

"What?"

Faith Edwards went on as if Linda hadn't spoken. "I didn't talk to those reporters when they came around in December. Bad enough we had to live with one tragedy without her coming back to stir things up again."

"Are you talking about Dorothy Miller's suicide?"

Faith Edwards nodded. Linda couldn't believe it. Was this woman saying it was Miller's fault for being overcome by despair so great that she took her own life?

Pete put a steadying hand on Linda's shoulder. "Do you know why she left town in '84?"

"It wasn't a secret. Everyone knew. It was the shame. The guilt."

"Guilt for what?"

"What happened at the old lighthouse. And Alfred Johnson getting killed because of it."

"How's that?" Pete asked.

"He was Miller's friend. Probably thought he was protecting her from what she brought on herself."

"Are you saying that was her fault too?" Linda could barely get out the words.

She'd seen it time and again in court. When all else failed, blame the victim.

Jed Whalen had said that the '84 case divided the town between those who believed Miller was having sex with multiple partners and those who believed she was assaulted.

Linda wasn't sure how that jived with Hank Bistrian's belief that Miller had been meeting someone, only to end up being raped.

But it was obvious that Faith Edwards was in the former camp.

"We heard that Mike Bonaker believed Miller was the victim of an attack," Pete said.

"He would, wouldn't he? She had him seduced too. Just like she seduced her stepfather. Everyone knew what Trask and Miller were doing. Then having sex with those boys while she was carrying on with another man. Should be a law against that. But what's really a crime is Bonaker letting that boy go. What kind of justice is that? Where's the justice for Alfred Johnson? Losing his life over a whore."

If Pete hadn't been holding onto her, Linda was sure she would have hit the other woman.

"Faith."

A voice floated down the stairs.

Faith Edwards stopped talking, as if she'd been caught doing something she shouldn't. But the anger was still there, in her hazel eyes and the hard planes of her angular face that hadn't softened with age.

Anger that had clearly been building for years.

She looked at Linda and Pete as if she were seeing them for the first time. "If you're doing a story, you should get it right this time. Let people hear the truth once and for all."

When Faith Edwards brought them into the bedroom, the first thing that hit Linda was the smell.

Antiseptic and musty as if it had been a long time since fresh air was let in.

Jesse Edwards looked pale and shrunken in the center of a hospital bed taking up a good part of the room. Scraggly wisps of white hair covered his otherwise naked scalp, and a morphine drip was in his left arm.

He looked from his wife to Linda and Pete as he tried to raise himself up on an elbow.

"No, Jesse." Faith Edwards came into the room, leaned down, and cranked up the bed.

"Stop fussing." Edwards lay back, the effort of moving exhausting him.

His wife hadn't budged from his bedside. "They want to talk about her."

"When are you going to stop?"

A look passed between husband and wife that Linda recognized. A look weighed down with all the accumulated baggage of a long marriage.

"Leave us," Jesse Edwards said.

"I'm not going anywhere."

"Faith."

She stood there with her arms folded. Although she was a slip of a thing, Faith Edwards exuded a strength that belied her slender frame. And there was the anger. Linda could see that she was a formidable woman when crossed.

"Ten minutes. I'll be in the kitchen if you need me."

"She wasn't always this way," Edwards said after his wife had left. He started to say more but erupted in a paroxysm of coughing that racked his emaciated frame.

After the coughing subsided, Edwards sagged back against the pillows.

"Can I get you something?" Linda asked.

"Water would be good." His voice was barely above a whisper.

Linda picked up the pitcher on the nightstand and poured water into the glass sitting next to it. Edwards drank like a man dying of thirst. After he was finished, he lay back against the pillows again.

"I heard you talking downstairs." He drew in a fortifying breath, but Linda could hear the rattle in his chest.

"First thing you need to know is I loved Dorothy Miller. Not the way you think. I loved her like a daughter. Faith and me . . . we were never blessed that way. It's part of why she—disliked—Dorothy so much. What she couldn't forgive me for. And I never could change her mind. Get her to understand how it really was. All I wanted was to protect Dorothy."

"From what?"

"The bad things in life. Dorothy'd had a rough time of it. Her father died when she was a kid. Mother worked in the local nail salon. Married to Lucas Trask, a fisherman who drank and had a vicious temper if you crossed him. Town gossips said Dorothy was sleeping with him. There were some wild rumors back then. Trask and Dorothy were going to leave Manatawkett and start a family. I never believed them. Always suspected Trask was abusing her. But Lucretia Miller believed her husband. Threw her daughter out. That was a sad day in Manatawkett. Dorothy had nowhere to go. I would have taken her in, but Faith would never have allowed it. Dorothy ended up moving in with Nancy Conklin."

"Who's Nancy Conklin?" Pete asked.

"She was Dorothy's best friend. Also waitressed at the yacht club."

His eyes suddenly welled up. "It was my fault. And then after Dorothy killed herself—" He shook his head, the tears flowing freely now. "If only I had it to do over."

"How was what happened to her your fault?" Linda asked.

"Because I didn't keep her safe. Couldn't protect her in my own kitchen."

"At the yacht club?"

As Edwards nodded, he was seized by another coughing spasm.

The door opened and Faith Edwards flew in. "I'm going to have to ask you to leave," she said as she poured more water into his glass.

But the spasm was already subsiding. "I told you, Faith . . . stop fussing . . . I'm . . . okay . . ."

"No, you're not. You in pain?" He shook his head, but she didn't believe him because she reached down and adjusted the drip.

"You've got five minutes," she warned Linda and Pete as she left the room.

"She's probably right outside anyway," Edwards said. "Nothing I'm telling you that she doesn't know. But she only dwells on the things she thinks I'm not telling her."

"She always thought the worst about us. But when a girl is as beautiful as Dorothy was, women are bound to be suspicious. Don't trust them. And don't trust their men around them. The men all wanted her. Her stepfather was no different. She'd come in for her orders, and I'd hear her telling the other waitresses about somebody at one of the tables harassing her. Married. Single. Old. Young. Didn't matter."

Edwards's eyes were starting to glaze over from the morphine.

Linda needed to keep him on track. "What happened in the kitchen?"

"He was a bad one. Worse than Trask. He'd been after her all summer. When I saw him in the kitchen that night, I was ready to take a knife to him. Would have too."

"Who are you talking about?"

Linda sent up a silent prayer.

Please don't let him be talking about Guy.

"Stuart Robbins."

Linda looked at Pete. The expression on his face told her that he was thinking the same thing.

The man Guy was suspected of murdering in a Manhattan hotel room had been in Manatawkett that summer?

"What happened?" Pete asked Edwards.

"Dorothy stopped me. I could see Robbins had been drinking. Had his hands all over her. I was ready to kill him. But Dorothy stood her ground, calm as you please, as if she was used to men pawing her. She told Robbins if he ever touched her again, she'd go to the police. That must have gotten through to him because he let her go. That was when I went over and shooed him out of the kitchen. Told him if I ever saw him here again, I'd go to the police. Know what he did? Laughed in my face."

Edwards took a sip of water. "After Robbins left, Dorothy was shaking so bad she could hardly lift her order off the counter. I told her I'd talk to the police and let them put the scare of Jesus in him. But she said I shouldn't interfere, that she could take care of herself. I shouldn't have listened. If I'd gone to the police, things might have turned out different. But she was afraid. Thought she'd lose her job. She made me swear I wouldn't. It shames me to say it, but I feared for my job too. I was assistant cook then. Moving up the ladder. Two nights later, she was assaulted."

"Did you see Robbins the night of the assault?" Pete asked.

"When I was on break out back having a smoke, I saw him with Douglas Beldock. Had their heads together, whispering. I knew they were up to no good."

"Who's Douglas Beldock?" Linda asked.

"He was Robbins's constant shadow. Never without a bottle. Didn't see him after that. But I saw Robbins."

"Where?"

"On the beach."

"When?"

"Just after eleven. Dorothy had gone off shift a few minutes earlier. I left the club, figured I'd put in an appearance at the bonfire. I saw Dorothy walking down the beach. That was when I saw Robbins."

"On the beach?" Edwards nodded. "Was he following Dorothy Miller?"

"I couldn't say for sure, but it seemed suspicious after what happened in the yacht club kitchen."

Linda took a moment to digest this second piece of information.

If Robbins had been following Miller, that could go a long way to placing Robbins at the scene. Together with what Edwards just told them, it would provide a motive for assault. Which meant that Robbins might have been involved in what happened that long-ago night.

Hank Bistrian said he saw Dorothy Miller walking down the beach around midnight.

Almost an hour after Edwards said he saw Stuart Robbins and Miller on the beach.

If Robbins had been following Miller, had she managed to get away from him, then gone on to meet her date?

"What about the boy who was found on the lighthouse roof?" Pete asked.

"The kid who was arrested." Edwards nodded. "The third one."

"Who was he?" Pete asked because Linda was suddenly having trouble breathing.

"Never knew. His name was kept out of the paper."

"Were Stuart Robbins and Douglas Beldock ever suspects?"

"If they were, no one knew about it. The whole thing was kept pretty hush-hush. I always thought it was because of their rich fathers. But the person to ask is Mike Bonaker. He was in charge back then."

Linda nodded. She planned to do just that, as soon as she and Pete found him.

"Did you tell Bonaker what you saw that night?" Linda asked Edwards.

"Yeah. He said he already knew about Robbins and Beldock."

"How? Who told him?"

"Never did find out. Maybe the kid Bonaker found on the roof. Or Dorothy. Though she never gave a statement. Left town a few weeks later."

That was interesting.

Why hadn't Dorothy Miller talked to the police? She was the most important witness. Not only to her own possible assault, but to murder.

Had she been threatened and was afraid of reprisal?

"What can you tell us about the kid who was killed?" Pete asked.

"Alfred Johnson. Golf caddy and ball boy at the club. Always following the city boys around. He was Nancy Conklin's boyfriend. They'd been going together since junior high school. Everyone figured they'd get married."

Edwards closed his eyes. He was starting to fade, either from the morphine or his illness, Linda couldn't tell.

"Thanks for talking to us, Mr. Edwards."

"Jesse," he said. "Please."

Linda and Pete were in the doorway when Edwards started speaking again.

"People forget Nancy Conklin was also a victim in all this. She suffered a terrible loss in '84. Had to relive it again when Dorothy Miller died. She took it hard. Started a fund for suicide victims in Dorothy's memory."

38

1984

When Guy walked into the house the morning after he and Dorothy had parted on the beach, his father was waiting for him in the living room.

Louis Kingship stood with his legs apart and his arms across his chest in an aggressive stance Guy knew well, demanding to know where his son had been.

Guy should have known.

Through the bedroom wall, he'd heard his parents arguing the night before.

No more trips to the library, Rachel. No more daydreaming on the beach, reading stories by dead authors. I'm not letting you turn my son into a pussy!

That morning, his face like thunder, his father told him to get his head out of books and start acting like a man. That he wasn't paying good money for nothing, and he expected Guy to clean the tennis court with the other kids by the end of the month.

Guy had already had two lessons, both miserable failures. He never could swing his racket back in time or run fast enough. He was glad Dorothy's waitressing shift hadn't started yet so she wouldn't have to witness him being humiliated again.

After missing the pro's serve—what else was new?—Guy watched the ball bounce onto the adjacent court.

"Well, if it isn't Guy Kingship. Read any good books lately?"

Guy looked up at the sound of a familiar voice.

On the next court, in expensive-looking tennis whites and the baseball cap that he never took off, Stuart Robbins was smirking at him.

On the other side of the net, also in tennis whites, a kid with floppy hair that he kept swiping out of his eyes glared at Guy. "Your ball's on our court."

Guy blinked, experiencing the feeling of dislocation that happens when people you know in one place suddenly show up in another. It was the shock of seeing Robbins and Douglas Beldock out of their natural habitat—high school—where they usually ignored him.

Unsure of what court etiquette demanded, Guy was looking to the pro for help when a tall kid in a blue-and-white striped shirt and khaki shorts ran onto the adjacent court. As he crouched down to retrieve the ball, which had come to a stop next to Beldock's sneakered foot, Beldock kicked it away.

Beldock and Robbins were still laughing as the kid in the striped shirt and khakis got down on his hands and knees in the tall grass to hunt for the lost ball.

An hour later, while waiting for his father to pick him up, Guy noticed a car parked across the lot.

And not just any car.

He'd never seen a Mercedes 380SL up close.

It was fire-engine red.

Guy couldn't resist walking over and checking it out. He peered inside at the dashboard and custom seats, wondering who owned the car and what it would feel like behind the wheel.

"Beautiful, isn't she?"

Guy turned around.

Stuart Robbins and Douglas Beldock were walking toward him. Beldock was holding a set of keys.

He should have known.

Beldock's father could have bought and sold their entire high school.

Robbins was wearing his usual smirk and baseball cap, which Guy had figured out was to hide his already thinning hair. "This baby's got a six-cylinder engine. Bet you'd kill to take her for a spin."

"No way," Beldock whined in his nasal voice. "I don't want any sissies in my Jag."

"Haven't I told you a thousand times, Dougie? You have to learn to share. You should feel sorry for Kingship. Ever see the heap of junk his daddy drives?"

Robbins turned back to Guy. "Meet us at the Overlook at nine o'clock tonight. Then you'll know what it's like to be in a real car."

39

1984

T his was like nothing Guy had ever experienced.

It felt even better than it looked.

The buttery smoothness of the custom leather in what passed for a back seat.

The smell of fuel and oil mixing with the briny tang of the sea coming in through the open windows.

The incredible smoothness of the ride. Guy could barely feel the road.

Not a single grind or rattle as Beldock shifted gears and the car picked up speed.

In the front seat, Beldock and Robbins were passing a whiskey bottle back and forth. As Beldock accelerated, Robbins shifted around and thrust the half-empty bottle at Guy.

He immediately thought of his father.

Robbins was still holding out the bottle, a challenge in his eyes. As if this were some sort of test.

Guy grabbed the bottle, chugged down the Scotch, and started coughing. Robbins laughed, and Guy felt his face grow warm. Robbins was still laughing as he took back the bottle.

A blind curve was ahead.

Instead of slowing down, Beldock floored the gas pedal, and the car shot forward.

"Slow down, Doug!" Robbins shouted. "You trying to kill us?"

Beldock laughed and gunned the engine, shifting gears again as he slammed around the curve.

Guy squeezed his eyes shut. Through the open roof, he could hear the waves crashing on the other side of the dune.

"Jesus, Mary, and Joseph!" Robbins bellowed. "You stupid prick! Didn't I tell you to slow down?"

Guy turned around. A car was on their tail.

"Bet it's a cop in an unmarked," Robbins said. "We're in for it now."

The other car was gaining on them, but the driver didn't pull them over. Instead, the car sped up until it was almost kissing their rear fender. Doug gunned the engine again to put some distance between them. The other car didn't have a tenth of their horsepower, but it was bigger and it accelerated as Beldock again shifted gears.

Guy felt the other car graze the bumper. Beldock went ballistic, shouting that if they touched his car again, they were dead. The kids in the other car just laughed and rammed them again. Beldock sped up, trying to get away from the other car, but he was going too fast and lost control, shooting across the divide and into the westbound lane—

—where another car was coming right at them.

Robbins screamed.

Beldock cut the wheel all the way to the right and swerved just in time. The car spun around and slammed into the shoulder, finally coming to a stop a few feet from a tree.

The three of them sat there.

Then Robbins started to laugh. Beldock joined in, followed by Guy, and soon all three were erupting in paroxysms of laughter.

When Guy sneaked into his room in the rental house later that night, careful to not wake his parents, he still felt the rush of adrenaline.

40

1984

D orothy's dark blue eyes searched his.

"Why do we have to keep our relationship a secret? It's because I'm older than you, isn't it?"

"No."

"You're ashamed of me."

"No! How can you say that, Dorothy?"

She bit her bottom lip. "Maybe I'm not good enough for you. Don't try to deny it. I've seen the way your father looks at me when I wait on your family at the club."

Guy's jaw clenched. "He has nothing to do with this."

"Doesn't he?"

The look on Dorothy's face made her suddenly seem much older. "You know he'd never let our relationship go any further."

"I told you, he has nothing to say about it!"

"I have to go. I have to get ready for work."

"Don't go away mad."

But she was already up and brushing the sand off her legs.

"Wait! Please. I love you. Dorothy!"

By the time he'd gathered up their things, she was halfway up the dune.

41

1984

When Guy met Dorothy on the lighthouse roof that night, she seemed to have gotten over her earlier anger.

But when he pulled her into his arms, he felt her resist.

Every time he tried to kiss her or show her how he felt, Dorothy got all weird and uptight, like those times in his parents' car.

When he pressed her for answers, she begged him to be patient. Then she started to cry. He couldn't stand to see her cry. It reminded him of his mother. She asked him to hold her, just hold her, and it took every ounce of willpower to keep from lifting her beautiful face to his and kissing her.

Tooling around in Doug Beldock's Jag was less complicated.

Less for Guy to have to think about.

Although he had to keep that a secret from his father as well. His mother too, because she worried about fast cars, citing all the accidents on the road, especially during the summer season, which was now in full swing.

◆

He'd just finished another god-awful lesson at the yacht club.

This time it was golf, at which he was even less proficient, unable to see the point of trying to get a ball into a tiny hole.

Dorothy was just starting her shift. Guy had seen her setting tables in the dining room for a brief moment when he arrived for his lesson. When their eyes met, he felt that same electric thrill he always did. Everything around him fading away, as if they were the only two people on the planet.

His father was visiting an old fishing buddy who lived in Amagansett, and Guy had told his mother that, after his lesson, he was having lunch with some new friends he'd made at the club. Afterward, he was getting a ride home from one of the boys, who was eighteen.

That wasn't a lie.

Doug Beldock was nineteen because he'd been left back and had to repeat his sophomore year. That meant he could buy the whiskey from Wolf's Liquor Store, a Manatawkett institution that had been around forever and was where everyone bought their alcohol.

Guy didn't tell his mother that his new friends were two boys he knew from high school who'd paid him zero attention before this summer. Or that one of them would always pull pranks that got him sent to the principal's office. Like the time Stu put a dead mouse in their homeroom teacher's desk.

Guy had less than three hours until his father returned for dinner.

After his lesson, he was leaving the yacht club with Stu and Doug when a voice called out. It was the kid from the club who was always trailing after the three of them.

"Your 380-SL is so cool," Alfred Johnson said to Doug, looking even more pathetic than usual with a bandage on his chin where he'd probably nicked himself shaving. "Must have cost a couple grand. I would kill to drive a car like that."

"Like I'm gonna ever let a loser like you touch her. Take a hike, ball boy."

Doug dangled his car keys in front of Johnson, then laughed as he and Stu strode across the parking lot, Guy as usual hurrying to keep up.

42

U p ahead was a hill. A pretty steep one, which Linda hadn't been able to glean from Google Maps.

They'd driven almost halfway up the hill when a roofline finally came into view. Followed by the house, which looked as if it were rising out of the air.

An optical illusion.

It was the thick vegetation surrounding the house that gave the impression. The place would be impossible to find if you didn't know it was there. Maybe Nancy Conklin preferred it that way.

Linda had found precious little personal information about her, except for the fact that Conklin had never married.

But there was a wealth of articles about Dorothy Miller's December 27 suicide that had dredged up the unsolved '84 murder.

Which only made things murkier. Now, as then, there were scant factual details about what led to the death of Alfred Johnson. Just a lot of wild supposition and unsubstantiated theories.

A few articles suggested that what happened at the lighthouse four decades ago was the reason Dorothy Miller came back and threw herself off of the roof.

To punish the town.

Nancy Conklin wasn't quoted anywhere.

"Maybe we should have called," Pete said. "I still can't get over the fact that Stuart Robbins was here in '84. Never saw that one coming."

Neither had Linda. Yet there it was. A connection between two murders that had taken place forty years apart.

And her husband was suspected of killing both victims.

A coincidence?

Except that Linda didn't believe in coincidences.

And once the Manhattan DA's office found out, they were going to have a field day. If they didn't already know.

In the past hour, Linda's phone had been buzzing nonstop. Mostly calls from the media, which she ignored.

But her heart leapt into her throat every time Pete heard about sightings of Guy or his car.

They turned out to be false alarms.

So far.

The case against her husband was speeding along. According to Pete's inside source, a subpoena had been issued to Guy's provider for his cell phone records for the days and weeks leading up to the murder of Stuart Robbins.

And just a few minutes ago, Diane texted to ask if Guy had gotten in touch and to let her know the minute he did.

Linda could have turned off her phone to avoid being tracked, although technically she wasn't doing anything wrong. But she was afraid to do that in case Guy called.

With every passing hour, that seemed less and less likely.

They'd reached the top of the hill. Linda could smell the water; caught a glimpse of Manatawkett Harbor. A dirt path wound around to a two-story, gray house that was in need of a fresh coat of paint.

Pete turned onto the dirt path, and the car bumped along until they reached the driveway. Pete killed the engine, and he and Linda got out of the car. They walked up the three steps to the porch, where a swing and a rocking chair sat opposite one another. An urn filled with bright red geraniums was next to the front door.

There wasn't any doorbell. Pete picked up the heavy knocker in the shape of an anchor and let it drop against the door, once, twice, three times.

Linda heard it echo through the house. A part of her was relieved when no one came to the door.

Maybe Pete was right. She shouldn't have come. But how could she stay in the dark? Live with the not-knowing?

Linda peered through the tiny window at the top of the door and saw a long hallway with a low-hanging chandelier. No sign of life inside.

She and Pete went around to the side of the house. The blinds on all the windows were drawn. Maybe Conklin was out back and hadn't heard them.

They walked across a flagstone patio that led to the yard, where there were two chaise longues and six chairs around a rectangular glass table and an aboveground pool stuck into the high grass like an afterthought.

When Pete knocked on the back door, no one answered.

"Maybe she's at the church brunch," he said.

Linda looked at her phone. "At two o'clock?"

"Today's Sunday. She could be visiting friends."

They followed the path around the other side of the house.

Linda stopped.

Vase after vase filled with flowers that looked freshly cut sat on two tables covered with white tablecloths. Hanging on the branches of a nearby tree were several pictures in ornate gold frames.

Linda walked up to the tree and studied the photos of a beautiful young woman with auburn hair and dark blue eyes posing in various settings.

The photographer had captured her astonishing, almost ethereal beauty. Also the deep unhappiness her lovely smile couldn't conceal.

This had to be Dorothy Miller.

In one photo, she was in front of the ocean wearing a red-and-black bikini and waving to the camera. In the background, the whitecaps of the ocean rose behind her, as if suspended in midflight.

In another photo, shot at a distance, Miller was a tiny figure in a windbreaker and sneakers standing at the bottom of a bluff. At the top of the bluff stood an imposing, once-white, weathered structure with a brown band around the middle and a black lantern at the top that looked to have been in disrepair even back then.

That must be the abandoned lighthouse.

Linda wondered why Nancy Conklin had chosen this particular photo. It had to be a painful reminder of how her friend had died.

Other photos shot in different scenic locations were of a man with brown eyes and a long face, displaying a goofy grin for the camera.

Alfred Johnson?

Nancy Conklin's murdered boyfriend.

As she gazed at the twin memorials, Linda couldn't imagine how Conklin had coped all these years, surrounded by death.

First, the loss of the boy she loved. Then her best friend forty years later.

Living a life shadowed by tragedy.

Something that Linda understood.

"You want to tell me what you're doing?"

43

L inda turned around.

A tall woman with a helmet of short gray hair stood there. She hadn't heard her come up behind them.

Linda tried to shake off the melancholia that had suddenly gripped her. "You must be Nancy Conklin," she said, smiling the charming, reassuring smile that usually won over reluctant witnesses.

Conklin didn't take the bait.

She stepped past Linda and Pete, who'd gone uncharacteristically quiet as he took in the poignant scene. Conklin turned and stood in front of the two tables, blocking the shrines from view as if Linda and Pete had committed a sacrilege. Then she reached into her straw bag and slid out a phone. "You have sixty seconds to tell me why you're here before I have you arrested for trespassing."

The woman didn't pull her punches.

"We don't mean to intrude on your privacy," Pete said. "We just need a few minutes of your time."

"For what?"

Conklin's tone thawed slightly as she looked at Pete, but she was still holding her phone. Her light blue eyes were set close together in a plain, square-jawed face. She was powerfully built, with broad shoulders. Her green sundress ended above a pair of tanned, muscular calves.

She looked as if she spent a lot of time outdoors. Gardening, if the fresh flowers that filled the vases were any indication.

"We'd like to talk to you," Linda said. "It won't take long."

"I don't talk to the papers," Conklin said. "Don't trust them. They twist every word you say."

"We're not reporters."

"Who are you?"

"We're writing a book about Manatawkett in the early eighties," Pete said. "We know about the ship that was lost at sea in '84."

They'd gotten that piece of information from Hank Bistrian.

"And secret government projects to develop psychological warfare that were conducted here," Linda added, as if they hadn't just come up with the idea once they Googled Manatawkett during that decade and uncovered a surprising treasure trove of facts.

"We wanted to include the unsolved murder of Alfred Johnson, which also took place in 1984," Pete said. "So far, we've gotten conflicting stories about what happened at the abandoned lighthouse back then and Dorothy Miller's suicide this past December. I apologize if it brings up unpleasant memories. I know how hard this must be for you."

"I don't need your sympathy."

"I understand." Pete nodded. "What can you tell us about Stuart Robbins and Douglas Beldock?"

If she was surprised to hear the names, Conklin did a good job of concealing it. "You want to tell me why you're asking about them?"

Whatever barriers Nancy Conklin had erected to protect herself, Pete and Linda definitely had her attention now.

"Sure," Pete said. "Do you mind if we sit down?"

Conklin hesitated. Then she put her phone away and led them to the glass table.

After they were seated, like friends about to share a companionable lunch, Pete introduced himself and Linda.

"We were told Robbins and Beldock might have been involved in an assault involving Dorothy Miller in '84."

"It's true. Those boys were pure evil. They deserved—"

"Deserved what?" Linda hadn't been prepared for the rage that ignited in Conklin's eyes. "How do you know Robbins and Beldock assaulted Dorothy Miller? Do you have personal knowledge?"

Conklin didn't answer right away, as if deciding how much to share with them. "I saw them."

"When?"

"That night."

Linda looked at Pete. "At the abandoned lighthouse?" she asked Conklin.

No one they'd spoken with so far had mentioned Nancy Conklin being there that night. Although Hank Bistrian did say that the beach had been crowded and it was impossible to tell who was coming and going.

"I saw them on the beach. Walking away."

As she studied Nancy Conklin, fury still darkening her eyes, Linda felt that familiar frisson of excitement she got when she was close to something concrete.

It wasn't evidence that could conclusively put Robbins and Beldock inside the abandoned lighthouse. Or prove they assaulted Dorothy Miller.

But she'd tried cases with less.

"I know it was a long time ago, but do you remember what time you saw Robbins and Beldock?"

Conklin shook her head. "I wasn't wearing a watch that night."

The way people kept track of time back then, Linda thought. Before cell phones put everything at their fingertips, including the ability to take photos and videos that might have captured something that could have been used as evidence.

"It was really late, though."

"How do you know?"

Conklin didn't answer. She turned away, but Linda could see her shoulders heaving.

"I was at the bonfire and starting to get worried about AJ—Alfred Johnson. He was my boyfriend. I hadn't seen him for a while. Then all of a sudden, there was this big commotion. Everyone started hurrying down the beach."

That must have been when word got out about a body going off of the lighthouse roof. Jed Whalen had told Linda and Pete that some kids who'd left the bonfire witnessed Alfred Johnson plunge to his death and called the police from their car phone.

When Conklin turned back to her, Linda could see emotion flickering behind the stony mask of the other woman's face. No doubt reliving the terrible night when her best friend was assaulted and her boyfriend killed.

"That was when I saw Robbins and Beldock. They probably thought they wouldn't be noticed in the crowd. But I saw them." She lifted her chin as if daring Linda to disagree.

But Linda was focused once again on the timeline.

Jesse Edwards said he saw Dorothy Miller and Stuart Robbins on the beach just after eleven. He couldn't be sure, but Robbins might have been following her.

Hank Bistrian claimed to have seen Miller headed down the beach around midnight.

That meant Miller was assaulted sometime after midnight.

Conklin said she hadn't seen Alfred Johnson for a while when she noticed Robbins and Beldock walking away from the lighthouse.

Johnson was the golf caddy and ball boy Jesse Edwards said had been following the city boys around all summer.

Had Johnson followed Robbins and Beldock to the lighthouse and witnessed the assault? Which would explain why Nancy Conklin saw Robbins and Beldock headed in the opposite direction after Johnson fell to his death.

Wrong place, wrong time, as some people believed, according to Jed Whalen?

"Did you tell Mike Bonaker what you saw that night?" Pete asked Conklin, who nodded.

That would be in the sealed record. Along with the statement from Jesse Edwards.

Who'd told them that Bonaker already knew about Robbins and Beldock.

From Nancy Conklin?

"What about the boy who was found on the roof?" Pete asked.

"What about him?"

Conklin's tone was challenging. Almost belligerent. And experience had taught Linda that when a witness answered a question with a question, it was usually because they were hiding something.

"We heard Dorothy Miller was meeting someone that night." Linda studied the other woman for the tells that would prove she was lying.

"Who told you that?" Conklin's expression had become guarded again, but she didn't look surprised.

Because she knew?

"Hank Bistrian," Pete said.

Conklin gave a scoffing laugh. "You mean the town drunk? Who's senile now? You can't trust a word that comes out of his mouth." Anger sparked in her eyes again.

"Was it the boy on the lighthouse roof?"

Conklin gave a vehement shake of her head. "Dorothy wasn't meeting Guy Kingship."

Hearing her husband's name spoken aloud for the first time was such a shock that Linda didn't immediately respond. "How did you know who he was?"

None of the three men they'd spoken with had known the identity of the boy who was arrested. And, according to them, the local paper hadn't mentioned any of the boys by name.

Conklin pushed back her chair. "I'm going to have to ask you to leave."

Linda dug in her heels. "Not until you tell me what you know about Guy Kingship."

"I don't have to answer your questions."

"Was Miller meeting him that night?"

"I told you, that's a lie!"

"Then how do you know who he was? If Miller didn't tell you?"

"I want you to leave. Now."

"Why was he arrested? You know, don't you?"

"You'd have to ask Dorothy. And she's dead."

"What did you tell the police?"

"How dare you try to interrogate me! Who are you, anyway?"

Nancy Conklin's eyes blazed with fury. For a second, Linda thought she was going to strike her.

But Linda stood her ground. She wasn't about to be intimidated by this lying, hateful woman with her decades-old anger and an axe to grind.

"I just want the truth."

"The truth," Conklin repeated, shaking her head. Then she looked Linda right in the eye.

"The truth is Kingship and his friends raped Dorothy and he killed my boyfriend. Now he's finally going to get the punishment that's coming to him. That's the story you should write. Now get the hell off my property, or I will call the police."

44

1984

"That is one hot chick."

"Wouldn't you like to get into her pants."

"Oh, I will. I can promise you that."

"Want to put your money where your mouth is?"

"I'll do better than that." Stu took a long swig from the whiskey bottle even though it was barely ten in the morning, then wiped his mouth with the back of his hand. "I guarantee you I'll have that bitch begging for it before the weekend's over."

Doug grabbed the bottle. "Fifty bucks says you don't."

"You got yourself a bet. It'll be like taking candy from a baby."

"Think she's a virgin?"

"You kidding?" Stu sneered. "She's a tramp, like all the local bitches. But I gotta admit, she is one of the finest-looking pieces of ass I've seen in a long time."

They were on the beach. Unusual to be here at this time of day. Guy had had to sneak out, now forced to miss his early morning encounters on the beach with the girl he loved. Those meetings had stopped ever since the beach started getting crowded and his father put the kibosh on it.

But Stu and Doug were never up this early. They barely made it to the yacht club for their tennis lessons and were usually hungover.

Now he knew why they'd gotten to the beach early this morning.

The three of them watched as the girl who'd just come out of the water removed her bathing cap and shook out her hair.

Her long, auburn hair.

Guy could barely think straight as he watched Dorothy walk across the sand to her towel. Stu and Doug were too busy ogling her to notice that he hadn't said a word. Part of him was still in shock; the other part was telling himself that he should have known.

Stu had noticed all the pretty girls in their high school. Guy had never figured out the secret of his popularity, but he usually had a new girlfriend every month.

Not only did Stu get the prettiest girls, but he was also famous for stealing other kids' girlfriends.

And now he was after Guy's girlfriend.

The question was, what was Guy going to do about it?

45

1984

When he got to the lighthouse roof that night, Dorothy wasn't there. Guy tried not to panic. It wasn't as if this hadn't happened before.

One time, another waitress at the yacht club went home sick and Dorothy stayed on past her shift to make some extra money.

And just last week, the night after she missed another date, she didn't offer an explanation. But she didn't say much at all. Barely broke a smile when Guy told her a joke to make her laugh. Something he would do with his mother after another terrible fight with his father. Guy didn't pressure Dorothy for details, wondering again what secrets she was keeping.

Their arrangement was no calls. Too risky, especially as there was only one telephone at the rental house and Guy couldn't take the chance that his father might answer.

But now, alone on the lighthouse roof on a perfect summer night, he couldn't stop the jealousy that was already rearing its ugly head.

Was it just a coincidence that Dorothy didn't show up tonight? Or had she noticed Stu on the beach and liked what she saw?

46

1984

The following afternoon, after a sleepless night, Guy still hadn't decided on the best plan of attack.

He tried to act as if nothing were wrong when he, Stu, and Doug left the steam room after another interminable tennis lesson where he missed nearly every ball the pro served to him.

He told himself that he just had to get through the rest of the day until he saw Dorothy tonight and cleared this up. He just hoped that she wouldn't be a no-show again.

Or he could confront Stu right now.

Tell him that Dorothy was off-limits.

But he had a feeling that wouldn't go very well. Was more likely to make things worse, in fact. And Stu hadn't said a word about Dorothy today.

Maybe he'd already set his sights on another girl.

Guy should have known better.

The three of them were in the parking lot headed for Doug's car when Alfred Johnson ran up behind them.

He'd been trailing after them all summer. No matter how badly Stu and Doug humiliated him, he kept coming back for more.

They were halfway across the lot when Stu suddenly whirled around.

"Quit following us, you creep."

"Why don't you make like Casper and disappear?" Doug made exaggerated flapping motions with his arms, trying to shoo Johnson away and laughing raucously at his own joke.

"You heard him," Stu said. "Get lost, ball boy."

Johnson stayed where he was.

"You're looking for Dorothy Miller, right?"

Stu stopped in his tracks. Turned around. Very slowly.

"What's it to you?" he asked Johnson.

"I heard you talking about her. I happen to know her roommate."

"Is that a fact?" Stu eyed him skeptically. "The operative question is, how well do you know her?"

"She's a friend of mine." Johnson puffed out his chest in a pathetic attempt to look important. "They both are."

"He's full of it," Doug said. "Come on. We're outta here." He already had his car keys out.

"It's true. I can prove it. I'll call her right now."

Johnson marched over to the pay phone and shoved a dime into the slot.

"Nancy? It's Al. I was just wondering if you and Dorothy are free tonight. Oh. Okay. Talk to you later."

He hung up, turned to the others. "She's working. Three-to-eleven shift. Dorothy too."

"What about after?" Stu asked.

"I didn't ask."

"Well, that was pretty stupid." Stu jabbed his index finger into Johnson's chest. "Call her back and tell her you've got something planned for later tonight. Tell her you'll pick them up at the club after they get off."

Doug advanced on him from the other side. "Think you can remember that, fuck-face?"

Johnson nodded.

"Why so quiet, Kingship?" Stu asked. "What's the matter, you don't like girls?"

"Maybe he doesn't think she's good enough for him," Doug sneered.

"She's good enough, believe me." Stu was still looking at Guy.

"Hey, Stuie," Doug said. "You holding out on me? You saying you already did her?"

"A gentleman doesn't fuck and tell." Stu winked at him. "Let's just say the lady's not indifferent to my charms."

"Nah. You didn't do her. Or you wouldn't be trying to get Johnson here to set it up."

"Oh yeah?" Stu whirled on Doug and slugged him.

Doug grabbed his face, letting out a high-pitched whine. "What was that for?"

"For doubting me, pea brain. Come on, let's get outta here." Stu started walking away, Doug right behind him.

47

"Nancy Conklin is one vindictive woman."

"With a real hard-on for Guy and the other two."

Pete rang the bell again.

Linda listened to the sound echo through the house, just like at Nancy Conklin's.

It was going on three.

After they'd left Conklin's house, they went back to the rental car to figure out their next move. When they passed the Manatawkett Community Church, Pete suggested stopping there to see if they could pin down a time when Mike Bonaker had left and where he might have gone afterward.

Turned out that Bonaker hadn't gone fishing but had stayed on after the brunch to lend an ear to some parishioners in need of more than spiritual guidance. They'd missed him by less than twenty minutes.

The minister, a Reverend Havens, was only too happy to give Pete directions to Bonaker's house, which wasn't far from the church. He told them that the Manatawkett chief of police had lost his wife to cancer the year before but was always ready to help those in need. He also reminded them that the church doors were always open.

Linda couldn't help feeling that the minister was speaking directly to her. As if he somehow knew that she'd lost her faith. And he would be right.

She'd stopped attending church after Mikey died, much to her parents' dismay. They, like others who'd suffered loss, had found religion to be a comfort.

She'd stopped doing a lot of things after her brother died. All the things a normal fourteen-year-old girl enjoyed that she no longer felt she deserved.

Because she was the reason her brother was out on that road in the first place.

Her parents never talked about it, but she could see the judgment in their faces.

She was an even harsher judge. When she convicted defendants, she wasn't only punishing the driver who'd fled the scene.

Linda felt as if the minister somehow saw all of that when he looked at her. As if he could see into her soul.

"Maybe Bonaker stopped to do some errands on the way home," Pete said. "Or help another parishioner in need."

"Let's give it a few more minutes," Linda said, forcing her mind back to the present. "He's the one we came to Manatawkett to see."

Their disturbing visit to Nancy Conklin had raised even more questions.

It seemed as if each person's account of what might have happened in '84 was contradicted by someone else's.

"We know Guy was on the lighthouse roof that night," Pete said. "And Conklin needed someone to blame for her boyfriend's death."

Linda nodded. "But the charges were dropped. Which means that Alfred Johnson was killed by either Robbins or Beldock. Probably Robbins, given what Jesse Edwards told us."

"We still don't know what Guy was doing at the lighthouse that night."

"Meeting Dorothy Miller."

Pete didn't say anything. Because he didn't believe that was true? Linda believed it.

The alternative was too terrible to accept.

"Something else that's bothering me."

"What?" Pete asked.

"Nancy Conklin's parting shot. That now Guy was going to get the punishment coming to him. Which means she knows that Stuart Robbins is dead. How does she know?"

"How does anyone know anything? She read it in the paper or saw it online."

"Could be," Linda said. "But I don't like it."

"What are you thinking?"

"I'm not sure. What I do know is she hated the three of them, Guy in particular."

"Jealousy?" Pete suggested. "Jesse Edwards told us how beautiful Miller was. Maybe Conklin was jealous. Or wanted Guy for herself."

"She already had a boyfriend," Linda reminded him.

"Doesn't mean anything." He looked at her, his eyes warming with an emotion she'd seen before. One that made no secret of his feelings, whether she was married or not.

Linda forced herself to look away.

"Another thing," Pete said, back to business as usual as if the previous moment hadn't happened. "If Miller came back to kill herself as a big fuck-you to the town, why wait almost forty years?"

"The anniversary?"

Linda was thinking about two other looming anniversaries.

The suicide of Guy's mother.

And the death of her brother.

So much tragedy. So much loss.

"Maybe we can get some answers now."

Linda turned around.

A car was pulling into the driveway.

48

1984

Dorothy was waiting for him when Guy pushed open the door to the lighthouse roof.

His heart galloped in his chest, the way it always did when he saw her.

A little later, as they sat close together and he stroked her hair, he brought up what had been on his mind ever since Alfred Johnson called her roommate from the pay phone in the yacht club parking lot.

The girl who was also Dorothy's best friend.

"You didn't tell anyone about us, did you?"

Dorothy shook her head.

"So Nancy doesn't know?"

"No. I swear. You made me promise. But I still don't understand why we have to keep our relationship a secret."

"What other things did you tell her?"

"About what?"

"So there's no one else?"

"Is that what this is about? You think—"

"What about Stuart Robbins?"

"What about him?"

"I hear the way he talks about you. He told Johnson to call Nancy and set something up for tonight."

"Do you see me with him? I'm here with you, aren't I?"

"But you like him, don't you? He was the coolest kid at our high school. He dated all the pretty girls."

"I don't care who he dates! Stuart Robbins is a class-A jerk. I'd never get involved with someone like him."

"Are you sure? Maybe you like somebody else. Everyone knows all the guys at the club have the hots for you."

But she'd turned away.

"D?"

When she turned back, her eyes were filled with tears. "I don't care about the other boys."

"Why me? I'm not cool like Stu."

"That's why I like you. Because you're not like him. I can't understand why you're friends with him and Douglas Beldock."

He had no answer for that.

The truth was, Robbins and Beldock had never paid attention to him before this summer.

Now he knew why.

Stu suspected he had something going with Dorothy. Maybe he thought he could use Guy to get close to her. And wasn't there a part of him that had secretly hoped Stu's popularity would rub off on him?

He felt ashamed now.

And how could he tell her that he liked driving around in Doug's expensive convertible?

Though lately Doug had been taking more and more risks.

The other day, they came a hair's breadth away from crashing into a tree. Stu threatened to take Doug's car keys away if it happened again.

"You're better than those boys," Dorothy said. "You're sweet and kind and smart. And—" She bit down on her lower lip. "I thought you were someone I could trust."

"I'm sorry, D. I was being stupid. Forgive me?"

She didn't answer, started twisting the heart-shaped locket she always wore around her neck. Jealousy blindsided him again as he wondered whether some boy in her high school class had bought it for her.

He grabbed her hands and forced her to look at him.

"You're the only one for me. You know that, don't you? Am I the only one for you, D?"

"You know the answer to that."

He pulled her closer. After a moment, he felt her relax in his arms.

"You know how I feel about you, don't you?" he whispered against her lips. "Show me you feel the same way."

"Guy—"

"Come on."

"No, Guy. Stop!"

He let her go. "What is it? Why'd you tell me to stop?"

"I don't want to be pushed. I told you, I'm not ready."

"But the summer's more than halfway over. When will you be ready?"

"It's not that simple."

"Yes, it is. If you're worried about protection—"

"It isn't that. I just—I need more time."

"How much time? I leave for college in September."

"I know. I'm sorry."

She was crying as she turned away.

49

H e was younger than she'd imagined, with alert, hazel eyes in a boyish face framed by a head of thick, gray hair.

Late sixties, Linda guessed. Which meant he hadn't been much more than a kid when he caught the '84 case.

Could mean something.

Could mean nothing.

Mike Bonaker wore a cop's typical poker expression as he walked toward them. As if strangers showed up unannounced on his doorstep every day of the week. "Heard someone was looking for me. Guess that would be you."

His voice had the disarming *You can talk to me, I'm your friend* tone that Linda often heard in cops trying to lull suspects into a false sense of security. But there was an edge to Bonaker's voice; a fine line of anger running under the surface.

Pete extended a hand. "I'm Pete Randolph and this is Linda Haley."

This was the first time they'd shared their last names. Not that anyone had asked.

Bonaker didn't take Pete's hand. "I know who you are."

The jig was up. Linda didn't know why she was surprised.

"I don't know what you were told," Pete said, "but is there someplace we could talk?"

Bonaker looked at Pete, who was looking at the glider, the only piece of furniture on the porch. It could seat one comfortably; two if they sat really close together.

Without another word, Bonaker pushed open the screen door.

They followed him into a dark house, where Bonaker flipped a switch on the wall, bathing the entry hall in muted light.

The house was silent, their footsteps the only sound echoing on the parquet floors as Bonaker led them deeper into the house. There were no signs of domestic life, no aroma of food cooking from the kitchen they were just passing, also bathed in darkness.

In the living room, Bonaker switched on a tall standing lamp.

Like the rest of the house, it felt stuffy. And sterile, Linda thought as she looked around. As if no one spent much time in here.

No books or art objects on the glass coffee table. A vase on the mantel over the fireplace was bare of flowers. The sofa was the only piece of furniture in the room that showed some homey touches, with its brightly colored pillows and the red, white, and blue crocheted throw blanket draped over one of the sofa arms.

Framed photos on a long, white lace doily lined the top of the piano. The keys were covered. Obviously, no one had sat down to play in a long time.

Linda couldn't resist glancing at the photos as they passed by, the one closest to her showing a younger version of Mike Bonaker. The woman on his right was smiling fearlessly into the camera. The young girl on his left bore a striking resemblance to Bonaker.

He saw where she was looking and glanced quickly away. But not before Linda saw sadness briefly shadow his face. As he motioned them to the sofa, she couldn't help wondering what kind of loss he'd suffered.

"Seems I'm very popular today," Bonaker said, once they were all seated, Linda and Pete on the sofa, the Manatawkett police chief on a tufted burgundy easy chair across from them. "Got the message a couple of hours ago. Was still in church."

He stretched out his long, gray-trousered legs. "I asked myself why the Manhattan District Attorney's office was calling me. Figured it had to be pretty important to reach out on a Sunday."

Bonaker looked at Linda. "Guess your boss doesn't know you're here, and I can understand why that's not something you'd want her to know. I have to say, though. It's a helluva thing, you being with the DA's office. Executive Assistant District Attorney. Isn't that right, Mrs. Kingship?"

Of course he would have been made aware of that fact as well. Especially when Linda happened to be the wife of the DA's prime suspect.

Who was currently MIA.

Bonaker's eyes were still on her. A cop's eyes. Measuring, sizing up. Missing nothing.

Linda had the feeling he was baiting her. Letting her know that he held all the trump cards.

Yet he'd allowed them into his house. That salient fact hadn't escaped Linda's attention, which told her that Bonaker was after something.

"What did you want to talk about?" he asked. As if he didn't know. But what did he expect in return?

"Since we're putting our cards on the table"—Linda leaned forward—"I need to know why you arrested my husband."

Bonaker scowled, now making no secret of his hostility. "I know you think I'm some clueless, small-town cop. And if you took a trip out here looking to clear his name, you came to the wrong place."

"The charges were dropped." Linda enunciated each word, feeling her own temper flare.

"That was then. And we both know there's no statute of limitations on murder."

The implication was obvious, even if she hadn't seen something in his eyes. "Are you saying you found evidence? After all this time?"

Newly discovered evidence was a rare occurrence, especially in a case this cold. But it happened.

The question was, had Bonaker shared whatever he'd found with the Manhattan DA's office?

"Way I see it, Guy Kingship got away with murder. Twice."

"If you mean Stuart Robbins, there's no dispositive evidence proving that my husband killed him."

"I wasn't talking about Robbins, though I was surprised to hear he was dead. He'd make it three."

"What the hell are you talking about?"

"Let's just calm down, okay?" Pete turned to Bonaker. "Who was the third victim?"

"Dorothy Hunter. That was her married name. But folks around here knew her as Dorothy Miller. The ones who remembered."

Linda stared at Bonaker, momentarily stunned into speechlessness.

"We were told she committed suicide," Pete said.

"That was the official cause of death. But make no mistake. Those boys killed her, same as if they'd pushed her off that light-house roof."

50

1984

When she was all cried out, Dorothy got up and walked across the roof.

"You're standing too close to the edge," Guy said. "Those railings aren't safe."

"How many feet up do you think we are?"

"A lot. A hundred and eleven, if you really want to know. Please, D. Come back."

Dorothy pointed at the observation tower. "You must have heard the stories about the lighthouse keeper who hanged himself. Do you know why? No one ever talks about that. One winter it was so cold, and his daughter got really sick. Influenza. His wife had died of the same illness the year before. It was just him and his daughter. After she passed, he didn't want to go on living. Could you blame him? She was his whole world."

Her voice had dropped lower. She could have been talking to herself as she stood at the railing, staring down at the ocean churning far below.

"As a kid, I always wondered. Why didn't he just jump? After he went under the waves, he might have floated away with the tide. Maybe his body would never have been found and he'd end up lying with the fishes, safe in the sea forever."

For a moment, he couldn't speak. Guy had never heard her talk like this.

"Dorothy, you're scaring me."

She blinked as she turned around, back from wherever she'd gone. "I'm sorry."

When she sat down next to him, he pulled her into his lap. "Everything's going to be all right," he said, because he didn't know what else to say.

He held her close, and she sighed and nestled deeper into him. He lifted up her hair to kiss the nape of her neck.

That was when he saw it. Not a hickey, made by some other boy. A bruise. As if somebody had had their hands around her throat.

Fury choked him.

Now he understood. Everything.

How could he have been so blind?

He, of all people?

"Who did this to you?"

"Guy, please."

"Who hurt you? Tell me!"

She didn't answer right away. When she turned back, she was crying again. "You have to promise me."

"What?"

"That we won't talk about this. Ever."

"But—"

"You have to promise."

His mother had said the same thing the day he first noticed the bruises. He was thirteen.

Guy begged her to go to the police. Rachel Kingship said it wouldn't do any good, that Louis Kingship was a powerful judge, so who would believe her?

He'd never told that to a soul, but now he found himself sharing it with Dorothy.

"How awful," she said when he'd finished. "No wonder your mother seems so sad whenever I wait on your family at the club."

Then she told him about her stepfather.

Guy listened in horror to the story of the nightly sexual assaults that began soon after Dorothy hit puberty.

Her mother told her if she went to the police, she'd say it was her daughter who'd seduced her husband. After Dorothy moved in with Nancy Conklin, she'd sometimes see her stepfather standing across the street, watching the house.

A few nights ago, he accosted her as she was walking to her car after finishing her waitressing shift at the yacht club.

"Why didn't you tell me this before?" Guy asked. "You can't stay here. It isn't safe for you."

"Where would I go?"

"Anywhere that isn't Manatawkett! What's keeping you here? A stepfather who rapes you and a mother who's jealous of you?"

"He'll find me."

"Not if we plan it right."

"We?"

"We'll run away together."

"That's crazy! You're sixteen! You're going to college in the fall."

"I don't care about college. I only care about being with you. We'll make our plans tomorrow night."

"Tomorrow night's the bonfire," Dorothy said.

"Even better. Everyone will be on the beach. We'll have the roof to ourselves." Tears stung his eyes. "I love you so much."

This time, when he drew her into his arms, she didn't resist.

"I love you too," she whispered into his neck. "You know that, right?"

He nodded, too overcome by emotion to speak.

She pulled away then, an intensity in her beautiful eyes. Her jaw tightened with resolve, as if she'd made up her mind about something.

"All that matters is the time we have left together." Then Dorothy leaned over and kissed him in a way she never had before and told him she was ready to give him what he wanted.

Guy wasn't sure he believed her, but he let her convince him that everything was going to be okay because he wanted her so badly.

As he held her close, his heart began to race.

Twenty-four hours from now, he would make love with the girl of his dreams.

Plan their future together.

He had no idea how he was going to survive until then.

51

"**C**an you tell us about the night Alfred Johnson was killed?" Pete was talking to Bonaker, but his eyes were on Linda. The reason they were here.

Anger and dread warred inside her.

"You mean after he witnessed Dorothy Miller being raped by Stuart Robbins, Douglas Beldock, and Guy Kingship?"

"My husband didn't rape or kill anyone."

"You ready to swear to that in court?" Bonaker asked Linda, daring her to contradict him.

"Can you walk us through what happened?" Pete jumped in again. "You got a call from some kids who saw a body fall from the roof of the old lighthouse, right?"

"Yeah." Bonaker reluctantly dragged his gaze from Linda. "Station was really busy. Always is the night of the bonfire. Had to make a couple of arrests. Petty stuff. Nothing anyone hadn't seen before. But soon as I got the call, I drove to the lighthouse. Found Kingship on the roof."

"What about Robbins and Beldock?" Pete asked.

"Didn't see those boys. Didn't know about them at the time. I only found out when Nancy Conklin told me."

"She told us she saw Robbins and Beldock on the beach walking away from the lighthouse that night."

"Told me the same thing."

"Did you question Robbins and Beldock?" Linda's voice was still tight with anger.

"Of course. They denied being there. Said they were at the bonfire all night. With all those bodies jammed together on the beach, there was no way to prove they weren't."

"What about Jesse Edwards? The cook at the yacht club?" Pete asked. "He told us he saw Robbins and Miller on the beach after Miller left the yacht club. At a few minutes after eleven."

"You really made the rounds, didn't you? Robbins denied that too. Said Jesse was mistaken. And it didn't put Robbins at the lighthouse that night. Or Beldock."

"Hank Bistrian said he saw Dorothy Miller headed toward the light-house almost an hour later," Linda said. "Sometime around midnight. He was convinced she was meeting someone."

"I heard that too."

"Why didn't you follow up? Bistrian said you didn't believe him, tried to make him think he was wrong about what he saw."

"I didn't try to do anything, and I resent your implying that I did. You don't know Hank. You couldn't trust anything he said when he was drinking. Which was most of the time. I didn't follow up because there was nothing to follow up."

"How do you know Miller wasn't meeting someone? That would explain why she was at the lighthouse that night."

"There's more to the story. Sure you want to hear it?"

52

1984

The night started out like every other night.

Coming into the dining room of the yacht club with his parents, eager as always for his first glimpse of her.

Spotting her as she came out of the kitchen, balancing a tray of dishes, her hair swept back from her face.

Staring as if seeing her for the first time, struck anew at her astonishing beauty, aware of the covert glances of every male in the room. Knowing that she was his—wanting to shout it to the world.

She's mine!

But tonight was different.

The plan was to meet after Dorothy got off her shift at eleven.

They'd debated putting in an appearance at the bonfire but concluded that it might be too hard to get away without drawing attention.

Better to stick to what they always did and go straight to the lighthouse.

Things started going wrong almost immediately. At dinner, Guy's father told him he had to attend a party some local politician was throwing, that he'd never get anywhere if he kept mingling with the hired help.

Which made Guy wonder if his father knew about him and Dorothy.

He looked around while Louis Kingship signed the bill, panicked when he didn't see her.

He made up an excuse that he had to go to the men's room. He found Dorothy at the bar, where she was filling a drink order, and told her about this new turn of events. He told her he might be late and she should wait for him on the lighthouse roof. He'd get there as soon as he could.

Dorothy was looking over her shoulder. She turned back to him with that slight widening of her beautiful blue eyes.

Her signal that it wasn't safe to talk.

Guy tried to appear casual as he turned in time to see the back of the hideous blue-and-green checkered sports jacket that Doug Beldock always wore. The yacht club was particular about their dress code.

At the party, Guy was forced to make small talk with a bunch of rich fat cats he'd caught ogling Dorothy more than once. The only saving grace was that he was able to sneak shots of the expensive Scotch that was flowing freely at the host's bar. If his father noticed, he didn't say anything. Guy wondered what Louis Kingship would think if he knew that his son had been on the sauce for weeks.

When Guy finally made his exit, he felt a bit unsteady on his feet.

The bonfire was well underway when he got to the beach, the acrid smell of smoke filling the night air. Loud voices and music almost drowned out the ocean, which was gentler tonight. Guy spotted other city kids he'd seen at the yacht club mingling with the locals as he passed, slowing to a walk so he wouldn't be noticed.

Once down the beach, he picked up his pace, ripping off his tie as he ran.

Guy's steps slowed. Told himself he was seeing things. It had to be the Scotch. He closed his eyes. When he opened them, Alfred Johnson was still there, standing a few feet from the lighthouse.

Blocking the entrance.

"What are you doing here?"

His words slurring a little. Must have been that last shot.

Johnson didn't answer, which only enraged Guy more.

"Did you follow me?" Guy looked around, half expecting to see Stu Robbins and Doug Beldock.

He turned back to Johnson.

"Get out of here."

The other boy didn't budge.

"Did you hear me?"

Johnson thrust out his lower lip. "You can't make me. You don't own the beach."

Guy couldn't believe it. Was he challenging him? Johnson never did that with Stu or Doug. He showed them more respect.

"Get lost, ball boy!"

Johnson cringed, and Guy felt a sudden, heady sense of power.

But Johnson stayed planted. "You're meeting someone, aren't you?"

That caught Guy off balance. Did Johnson know?

Guy tried to think past the haze of alcohol. In his mind's eye, he saw the back of Doug Beldock's sports jacket as he and Dorothy whispered together at the yacht club.

Had Alfred Johnson somehow gotten wind of their plans?

Or maybe he heard it from Nancy Conklin, who got it from Dorothy, her roommate and best friend, even though Dorothy had sworn to Guy that nobody knew about their relationship.

Guy gave Johnson his fiercest glare. "I'm counting to three."

"What are you going to do? Hit me?"

Guy was totally flummoxed.

He'd never see Johnson like this. He was usually so meek and subservient.

And every minute he stood there kept Guy from being with the girl he loved.

Guy wasn't aware that he'd begun advancing on Johnson until the other boy started backing up, brown eyes huge in his long face.

Then he turned on his heel. And ran.

53

There was a long silence after Bonaker finished talking.

Linda kept seeing Guy standing in front of the railing at the edge of the lighthouse roof, where Bonaker said he'd found him, staring down at the ocean where Alfred Johnson's body had just been discovered.

"Doesn't prove he pushed Johnson off," she finally said, her words sounding weak to her own ears. Lacking conviction. Like every defendant she prosecuted.

"Really?" Bonaker gave her a look that told Linda he saw right through her. "What about Kingship's busted jaw? The shiner under his eye? Think he did that to himself?"

"Doesn't mean it was Johnson. It could have been Stuart Robbins. Or Douglas Beldock."

"Then why didn't Kingship tell me that?"

"You said it yourself. He couldn't remember what happened up there."

"Convenient, isn't it? Or maybe you're right. It wasn't Johnson who slugged him. It was Robbins or Beldock because they wanted their turn."

"How dare you!"

Pete jumped in before Bonaker could respond. "You haven't told us why the charges were dropped."

The anger that flared in Bonaker's eyes matched what Linda was feeling. "His father, that's why. When I brought Kingship Jr. into the station, he refused to talk until Kingship Sr. got there. Had enough wits about him to say that. And the kid had been drinking. I could smell the whiskey on his breath a mile away."

"What happened?"

"Louis Kingship went over my head, straight to the Manatawkett police chief, Greg Karlin. My boss at the time. The next day, I was told that the Suffolk County DA was dismissing the charges. I couldn't believe it. I had Kingship dead to rights on that roof. Had motive too. There was an argument between Kingship and Alfred Johnson in front of the lighthouse that night."

This was news to Linda. "How did you know about this alleged argument between Johnson and my husband?"

"There was a witness to the altercation. A kid who was passing by."

Not what Linda wanted to hear. "So far it's all circumstantial."

"You mean there's no smoking gun? How many cases have you prosecuted when the murder weapon was discovered in the defendant's hand? We not only had enough for probable cause to make that arrest, we would have gotten an indictment if the case had gone to a grand jury. Instead, Kingship and his friends got off scot-free, and we were left with the mess they created."

"What about Dorothy Miller?" Pete said. "We heard she never gave a statement. That she left town."

"Because the three of them threatened her."

Linda's anger reignited. "You have evidence of that? Or are you still trying to twist the facts to fit your theory of what happened?"

Bonaker glared back at her. "Except that now Kingship's done it again. And he's on the lam. Innocent people don't run. Tell your husband to turn himself in. You know how the DA's office works. It isn't too late to make a deal."

This was what Bonaker was after. Tell a story that incriminated Guy so Linda would convince him to surrender.

That meant Bonaker had evidence.

Which he would try to match to Guy once he was arrested and compelled to give a DNA sample. Even though Guy had been arrested in '84, the charges had been dropped before Bonaker could get physical evidence.

"Your plan could backfire if your evidence points to Stuart Robbins. You can't arrest a dead man."

Her comment had hit home. Bonaker frowned, which gave Linda hope and confirmed for her that he did have some kind of evidence.

"We know Dorothy Miller was meeting someone because even if Hank Bistrian got it wrong"—Linda's tone let Bonaker know that she didn't believe that for a minute—"the fact remains that Miller was at the lighthouse that night."

"Okay. Let's say you're right and Miller was meeting someone there. Let's say it was your husband. Miller thinks it's a date."

"You make it sound as if it were something else. As if my husband lured her there under false pretenses. Did it ever occur to you that their meeting was completely innocent?"

"Next you'll be telling me that Miller and your husband were having a relationship."

"How do you know they weren't?"

"Answer me this, then. If they were involved, how come no one knew about it?"

She had no answer for that. "Maybe they didn't want anyone to know."

Guy's father? Linda wondered.

City and local kids not mixing?

Bonaker shook his head. "You can sugarcoat it all you want with romantic theories. But you're the one who needs to face facts, Ms. Haley. And those facts are that your husband's the one who was arrested in '84. Now he's wanted for murder again. From where I'm sitting, it looks like history's repeating itself."

54

The sudden cloud cover that obscured the sun had turned into a fog, creating pockets of mist as they drove to the beach. The fog was so thick it was hard to see the ocean. Only the tips of the whitecaps were visible as they crashed into shore.

Linda walked along the beach, carrying her shoes, feeling the sand shifting under her feet. She hadn't been on a beach in decades, since after her brother died and her father sold his family share in the house at the Jersey Shore. Then she married Guy, who had a dread of anything having to do with the ocean.

She'd thought it was because of his mother's suicide. Now she knew differently.

What she didn't know was if her husband had done these terrible things—something she'd never admit to anyone. She could barely admit it to herself. But the longer Guy was AWOL, the more doubt, like the fog, was creeping in.

Linda didn't like doubt. It was a prosecutor's enemy. If there was one thing that she'd always been sure about, it was that every defendant was guilty.

Do you ever wonder if they're innocent? Guy had asked at breakfast a few weeks ago.

Not a chance, she'd replied.

In this instance, the only one who could tell her the truth was her husband. And she had no idea where he was.

Her boss didn't believe that. Diane had texted twice in the past hour. In a way, Linda couldn't blame her. How many cases had she tried where spouses or partners possessed no knowledge of the defendants' whereabouts? Weren't complicit in some way?

Not many.

Diane's last text was more disturbing, although not completely unexpected. She wanted Linda to know that they were gathering evidence against Guy, and an indictment could be imminent.

Even if he remained off the radar.

What most people didn't know was that a grand jury could indict a defendant in absentia.

Because a grand jury was the district attorney's show. Defendants could only testify if they were given the green light by their attorneys, who weren't permitted to call or cross-examine witnesses.

Now Linda was starting to understand how it felt to be on the other side. And her window of time to find answers was starting to close.

The sea was getting louder. Mist dampened her skin.

As she walked, Linda tried to distract herself from what was going on in the present by picturing Dorothy Miller hurrying down this same stretch of beach forty years ago. Trying to get away from Stuart Robbins, as Jesse Edwards had intimated.

Which Miller must have done, because Hank Bistrian saw her almost an hour later once again walking down the beach. He was sure that Miller was meeting someone after having bought lipstick and perfume in his general store that same afternoon.

Linda could almost see Dorothy Miller now, wearing the new lipstick. Her perfume drifting on the night air as she hurried to the lighthouse. Not in fear this time, but anticipation.

Because she was meeting someone.

Guy?

Why the lighthouse?

A place where they could be alone? And with everyone at the bonfire, no one would know they were there?

Except Stuart Robbins.

Had he picked up Dorothy Miller's trail again after she thought she'd shaken him? And this time, Douglas Beldock was with him?

A scream pierced the air. Linda looked up, and through the mist, she could make out a lone seagull circling above.

She kept walking.

And suddenly, there it was.

Rising out of the fog like a towering white apparition, the black lantern at the top barely visible.

The scene of the long-ago crimes.

As Linda approached the bluff, she saw that time had not been kind to the building, now a deteriorated husk of what the lighthouse must have once been.

Yet it was still standing.

The path leading up to the top of the bluff was a rocky sandbank, making the climb a treacherous one. And there were warning signs on placards dug into the sand, which Linda ignored.

She walked past the NO TRESPASSING! DANGER! KEEP OUT! signs and approached the lighthouse door.

That hadn't aged well either, the steel rusted and wood joints corroded from more than a century of exposure to water and salt air.

There was a broken lock on the door. The lock looked relatively new.

Linda wondered if the lock had been placed on the door as a deterrent after Dorothy Miller's suicide. It obviously hadn't discouraged voyeurs who wanted to visit the scene of yet another death.

Despite the broken lock, the door didn't give easily. When she finally managed to heave it open, the momentum sent Linda stumbling backward. As she regained her balance, something big and black flew out of the lighthouse.

She whirled around, watched it sail out over the ocean until it merged with the darkness, then she turned back to the lighthouse.

A smell was wafting out, of damp and rot and neglect. Holding her breath, Linda aimed her phone light inside—she didn't want any more surprises—but all was darkness within.

The interior of the lighthouse was surprisingly cool. Cobwebs brushed her face, and Linda impatiently peeled them away and once again aimed her phone light.

A set of green spiral stairs came into view.

She trained the light on the steps' winding, upward arc, the bright white beam dispersing the shadows overhead until it looked as if the darkness itself was moving. Flying straight at her.

A deafening sound filled the lighthouse as they swooped down, Linda ducking just in time. She crouched down, overcome by the stench. There was more flapping as the bats flew out, looking like one long plume of smoke.

She rose slowly to her feet, cobwebs still clinging to her.

She shone her phone on the dark corner under the stairs and remembered Hank Bistrian saying that some people in town believed Dorothy Miller had been assaulted there. Linda shivered and told herself it was from the dankness as she tried to reconstruct the sequence of events.

If Miller had been raped down here, how did Guy end up on the roof with Alfred Johnson's body floating in the ocean more than a hundred feet below?

What happened during that critical period of time between the assault and the murder?

Linda walked to the green spiral steps.

You don't have to do this, she told herself.

But of course she did. She had to see it for herself.

She started to climb, slowly because the rusted iron steps were narrow and uneven, her mind continuing to buzz with questions.

Had Dorothy Miller been meeting Guy here that night, despite Nancy Conklin's insistence that she wasn't? Again, she asked herself how Conklin could be so sure that Miller wasn't meeting Guy.

And why was Linda so sure that Conklin had been lying?

As she climbed, she could hear them through the open windows she passed on her way up. Seagulls. There were more of them now. They sounded as if they were circling the lighthouse, their cries almost drowned out by the roar of the sea.

The ascent was growing steeper, and her heart pounded against her ribs. Linda stopped to catch her breath. She felt winded, which she suspected was less from physical exertion than from anxiety.

She could use some water, and she mentally berated herself for coming here without a bottle. The last thing she could afford was to become dehydrated, especially in her condition.

Coming to the lighthouse had been an act of impulse. Like driving to Manatawkett to find out what secrets Guy had been concealing from her throughout their entire marriage. Not her typical, carefully thought-out planning. But nothing about her life was typical now.

And she still clung to the belief that uncovering the truth about Guy's past would help shed light on the present crime.

And exonerate him.

One more set of stairs to go. As she started climbing again, Linda tried to avoid looking down. That would only make her dizzy and likely bring on another onset of nausea.

When she finally reached the top, she let out a relieved breath, only to feel anxiety return as she stood in front of the door.

Was this how Guy felt when he had the recurring dream of standing in front of a door?

Except that he knew what lay on the other side of his parents' bedroom on the second floor of their Manhattan townhouse. Even if he'd buried the physical memory deep in his psyche.

She knew that she was being ridiculous. There was no one here. Just her and the seagulls.

She'd always prided herself on being a woman of action, and she hadn't come this far to turn back now.

The hinges creaked as Linda pushed open the heavy door and walked outside.

55

Even with the low-lying fog, she could see that the roof was empty. What had she expected? A place populated by the ghosts from her husband's past?

Linda forced her feet to move, recalling Jed Whalen saying that local groups had been lobbying to tear down the lighthouse for decades. Calling it a death trap.

She could see why.

The low iron railing encircling the roof that had been designed as a protective barrier more than a century earlier had disintegrated into a pile of metal that offered precious little separation from the edge.

Linda made her careful way across the cracked, uneven stone that was slippery with moss.

She stopped several feet from the edge, took a steadying breath, and looked down.

Was she standing in the same place where Mike Bonaker had found Guy, staring at Alfred Johnson's body in the water?

Linda couldn't see the ocean at all now. But she could hear its ceaseless pounding.

Bonaker said that Guy had had a shiner and his jaw looked as if it had been busted. Had an altercation that began in front of the lighthouse ended with Guy pushing Johnson off of the roof?

What had they been arguing about?

Why did Dorothy Miller come back here forty years later to take her own life?

More questions without answers. And she wasn't going to find them here, at a decades-old crime scene.

If any evidence had been left up here, it was long gone. Except for whatever Mike Bonaker had discovered.

Bonaker's voice floated out of the mist.

Innocent people don't run.

Maybe it was the heaviness in the air, but once again, Linda had trouble catching her breath.

She had to get out of there. Had to get away from this cursed, haunted place that felt as if it were rotting from the inside out.

A silent witness to two violent deaths.

Three, if you counted the original lighthouse keeper, who'd hanged himself in the observation tower in the center of the roof. Now a decayed hulk with its cracked stone, warped wood, and blacked-out windows.

It took every ounce of self-control to stop herself from running.

She had never been one given to flights of fancy, but as she walked back across the roof, Linda imagined that she could hear the voices of Alfred Johnson and Dorothy Miller.

Clamoring for justice.

She pulled open the door.

The descent was more treacherous than climbing up had been.

With one hand grasping the rusting iron railing that was slippery in her clammy hand and the other hand placed protectively on her belly, Linda forced herself to climb down slowly.

When she emerged from the lighthouse, the fog was so thick she couldn't tell where the sea ended and the sky began.

As she walked away, she thought she heard her name being called.

Pete materialized out of the mist. She'd left him where they'd been sitting together on the sand after she told him she needed to take a walk to clear her head.

Alone.

Not consciously aware of where she was headed until she was halfway down the beach.

Now she watched Pete hurrying toward her across the sand; a marked contrast to his usual confident, unrushed stride.

"What is it?"

Linda could barely hear her own voice under the thunder of the surf.

Pete was breathing hard as he ran up to her, the light from his phone reflecting his shocked expression.

"I started thinking, what if we were looking at the wrong person for Alfred Johnson's murder. And it wasn't Stuart Robbins? Douglas Beldock was also at the lighthouse that night. He could have been the one who pushed Johnson off of the roof. But if he did kill Johnson, we're never going to know."

Linda looked at him.

"Douglas Beldock's dead."

56

They'd been on the road almost three hours.

Hard to believe they'd left Scarsdale for Manatawkett only this morning. To Linda, it felt like another lifetime. She was still trying to process the fact that two of the rapists were dead.

Which was sure to confirm Mike Bonaker's belief that Guy was responsible.

The only one left.

There would be no help from Bonaker, especially after the earful he must have gotten from the DA's office.

Linda could just imagine how that conversation went.

And if her earlier suspicions were correct, Bonaker had gotten hold of a piece of damning evidence. Something that could point the finger at Alfred Johnson's killer forty years after the fact. Some kind of blood evidence. Like DNA.

Then there was Nancy Conklin. Linda was convinced that she was hiding something. Whatever it was, she'd buried her secrets deep. But not her hate.

"Conklin's lying."

"About what?" Pete put on his blinker and moved into the left lane. Everything?

"You were there. You heard the way she talked about Guy and the other two."

"Are you thinking she knows something? Or she's involved in some way? So far, there's no evidence that Douglas Beldock's death Saturday night was anything other than an accident. He was drunk, went off the road and crashed into a tree."

"The timing's too suspicious. Nancy Conklin's got to be the one behind this."

"We have no proof of that."

"You said it yourself, Pete. She hated the three of them, especially Guy."

Linda had just thought of something else. "Remember when Conklin was talking about Robbins and Beldock? How she started to say they deserved—something? At the time, I thought she meant they deserved to be punished. And that it hadn't happened yet. Except she knew that Robbins was dead. But how did she know Beldock was?"

Pete shrugged. "Same way she found out Stuart Robbins was. She read about it."

"There's another possibility. She knew they were dead because she's the one who killed them. That's why she didn't finish her sentence. She was afraid she'd give herself away."

"So this is all about revenge?"

"Right. And Dorothy Miller's suicide was the catalyst. You saw the shrine at Conklin's house. Jesse Edwards said she took Miller's death hard. Even started a fund in her memory."

"So, what? Conklin ran Beldock off the road?"

"How hard would that be? Especially if he was three sheets to the wind."

"And Stuart Robbins?"

"That's more complicated because Conklin needed to frame Guy for Robbins's murder. Just like he was arrested for Alfred Johnson's murder."

"Bonaker said no names were ever released."

"Nancy Conklin had to know that Guy was the one arrested because she told us he killed Johnson. That's why she tried to deny Dorothy Miller was meeting Guy at the lighthouse that night when I asked. In her mind, if Miller and Guy had been seeing each other, that made it less likely that Guy was one of the rapists. Which meant he would have had no motive for killing Johnson."

"But why Guy?" Pete asked. "Why not Robbins or Beldock? Conklin told us she saw the two of them heading away from the lighthouse after Johnson went off the roof. Even Bonaker isn't sure which of the three killed him."

"Because Nancy Conklin hates Guy," Linda said. "And he's the one who was found on the roof. Which made him the perfect patsy. Now Conklin's trying to make history repeat itself. Just like Bonaker said. But it's her vendetta, not Guy's."

It all made sense now.

"That was why Conklin needed the woman. To lure Guy to the hotel room." Linda felt Pete's eyes on her as she kept talking. "The witness you told me about said he saw a woman outside the hotel room. And she hasn't been seen since. Convenient, isn't it?"

"So this woman was Conklin's accomplice."

She couldn't believe that he didn't get it. Or didn't want to.

"Conklin couldn't be the one to set up Guy. What if he recognized her?"

And Nancy Conklin would have been too old. The woman who seduced her husband was young. And beautiful.

"This accomplice. Didn't she know what she was getting into? And the room was reserved in Robbins's name."

"She could have lured Robbins there too. Gotten him to book the room. Playing both sides. The witness saw the woman outside the hotel. She never went into the room. Maybe Robbins was already dead and Conklin was inside waiting to ambush Guy. She knocks Guy out, plants his phone. Guy wakes up in a room with a dead body. Conklin is the one who makes the anonymous call to nine-one-one. But Guy gets away before the police show up."

"And the woman?"

"Long gone. She did her job. Even if she read about the murder after the fact, it was too late. She wasn't going to come forward even if she felt guilty. Not when she could be charged as an accomplice."

"One problem with your scenario. There's nothing to put Nancy Conklin or anyone else in that hotel room. The only physical evidence belongs to Robbins. And Guy."

"That's why we need Douglas Beldock's car. If Conklin ran him off the road, she might have left evidence behind."

Pete's silence spoke volumes.

"You don't believe it's Conklin, do you? And Robbins and Beldock dying within twenty-four hours of each other is just a coincidence?"

"There's another possibility, but you're not going to like it."

"What? That my husband is a rapist and a three-time murderer? Who the hell's side are you on, anyway?"

Linda rolled down the window. The AC was going full blast, but she was suddenly having trouble breathing. She needed air, and her stomach was roiling like crazy.

"Linda? What's wrong?"

"I need to get out."

"An exit's coming up in less than a quarter of a mile. Should be a rest stop."

"I can't wait. Stop the car. Now."

He didn't need to be told twice. Within seconds, he'd maneuvered back into the middle lane, then into the right lane.

Linda already had the passenger door open when Pete pulled onto the shoulder. She ran from the car, her stomach rebelling with every step. Trees and underbrush curved steeply down to a large ravine. Dizziness assailed her as she looked down. Hands on her knees, she bent over double and took in shuddery breaths of fresh air until the nausea finally passed.

"You okay?"

She felt Pete's arms on her shoulders and shook him off. Another wave of dizziness hit her. This time, when he reached out to steady her, she didn't push him away.

"Does Guy know?"

She should have expected that. She never could hide anything from him.

Linda shook her head and buried her face in his chest. He wrapped his arms around her tighter. Then she was crying, sobbing as if her heart would break.

When she was all cried out, she pulled away and swiped at her damp face. "I'm sorry."

"There's nothing to be sorry about. You're under a tremendous strain."

Their eyes met as crickets chirped in the distance. She had no idea where they were. It felt like the middle of nowhere.

Then she was in his arms again, thinking how tired she was of having to be strong, how nice it would be to have his broad shoulders to lean on for a change. That it had to be the hormones because suddenly all she could think about was kissing him, wanting to kiss him more than she'd ever wanted to kiss anyone in her life, and if she cheated, it couldn't be with anyone but Pete, who loved her and whom she loved a little too, and how liberating it would be to behave irrationally for once, to throw caution to the wind, let everything go, feeling nothing but Pete's strong arms around her.

57

"Am I crazy, Pete?" Linda asked once they were back on the road. "Grasping at straws?"

"I honestly don't know. But are you prepared to accept the truth? Whatever that turns out to be?"

That was the question.

She, who pursued every case to the bitter end, all in the name of justice.

But in this instance, her argument supporting a connection between the deaths of Douglas Beldock and Stuart Robbins was a double-edged sword.

One that could give Guy motive. That presupposed he'd known about Dorothy Miller's suicide and was afraid that if the Johnson cold case was reopened, Beldock and Robbins might talk.

But if Guy had been trying to silence the other two, he would have to have known that Stuart Robbins would be in the hotel room Friday night. It would mean that it wasn't Nancy Conklin but Guy who conspired with the woman to lure Robbins there.

Guy who ran Douglas Beldock off the road.

Was he capable of that kind of cold-blooded premeditation? She didn't want to believe that. But she couldn't ignore the facts.

Fact number one: Guy had been arrested for the '84 murder. He was the only one charged.

Fact number two: two men—possible rapists and witnesses to Alfred Johnson's murder—were dead.

Those were the facts.

The first thing you learn as a lawyer is not to let emotions cloud your judgment.

But this was her husband, for god's sake. Who had been behaving erratically for months. Longer than that, if she were being honest with herself.

Wasn't that why she married him? Because he was damaged? Because he needed her?

And she needed to feel needed. To succeed where she had failed.

To make amends.

To be forgiven for that which was unforgivable.

Until Guy committed the cardinal sin of no longer needing her—or so it had seemed—stuck in a job he hated but refused to talk about. Retreating deeper into himself, closing himself off in his den with his Scotch and God knows what else.

Her response? To bury herself in her work. Or had it been the other way around?

All she knew was that the more shut out she felt, the more she, too, retreated. She found an outlet in her career—protecting victims by convicting the men accused of their rapes and murders.

Had Guy committed these crimes? Was that her fault too, for not being more vigilant? For failing to keep him safe, just as she failed her brother?

She was supposed to be babysitting him that afternoon, but she was too busy gossiping with her girlfriend on the phone to notice that Michael had gone into the garage, eager to ride the bicycle their parents had bought him for his tenth birthday.

He was hit by a car half a block from their house.

Every time she convicted a defendant, she was also punishing herself.

Guy had been her shot at redemption, her penance for Mikey's death.

And now it could be too late.

"Linda?"

Pete was waiting for her answer.

She looked at him. His hazel eyes were bright with emotion, no longer trying to hide his feelings.

Feelings that a part of her shared. And she'd almost given in earlier, had pulled away at the last minute.

"I'm scared," she said.

Pete had one hand on the wheel and reached for her hand with the other.

Linda didn't say anything more, but she'd made up her mind. She couldn't remain in the dark.

Even if the evidentiary trail led back to her husband.

58

The sun was a red fireball on the horizon when Pete pulled into the parking lot of the Hartford PD at eight-twenty-five Sunday night. Douglas Beldock had lived most of his adult life in this scenic Connecticut town.

And he'd died here.

After they were seated, the detective who'd brought them into his office cut right to the chase. "What can I do for you?"

Pete handed him his card. "Anything you can tell us about Douglas Beldock's death?"

Detective Donovan looked at the card, then at Pete. "Mind telling me why? You're a bit of a hike from New York City."

"It's in connection with a case we're investigating."

That was the standard response cops always gave when they wanted information.

The Hartford detective gave no indication that he suspected their visit to be anything other than what it seemed. But with Guy still

AWOL and the threat of an indictment hanging over him, Linda really felt now as if she were in a race against time.

"Don't know that there's much I can tell you," Donovan was saying. "Pretty open and shut as far we can make out right now. I hate to speak ill of the dead, but Beldock's death didn't come as that much of a surprise."

"I know Beldock's license was revoked last year after he was arrested for a second DUI."

Pete had uncovered those facts during the interminable drive here.

"In Connecticut, we call them OUIs," Donovan said. "Operating Under the Influence. Same thing. In Beldock's case, he was a ticking time bomb. Which isn't to say that what happened isn't a tragedy, but he should never have gotten his license back. He'd probably still be alive. Worst part is we see a lot of fatalities like this, and the drinking and driving is only getting worse. Laws need to be a lot tougher."

Donovan gave them a smile tinged with sadness. Linda wondered if he was speaking from personal experience.

"Pet peeve of mine. Wish I could have been of more help. Sorry you came all this way."

He rose from his chair, indicating that their brief conversation was over.

"Do you mind if we take a look at the scene of the accident?" Linda asked.

Donovan looked at her for so long that she wondered if he'd sussed them out after all. Finally, he nodded.

"Sure. It's not far."

It was a ten-minute drive from the station.

As the three of them walked to an area that had been cordoned off, Linda was aware of a familiar tug of excitement. She often felt in her element at a crime scene.

Except that she had a hell of a lot more than usual riding on this one.

Donovan stopped at a roped-off area in front of an enormous tree. He shook his head as he indicated the tree.

"It's a wonder she's still standing. This isn't the first time she's been hit, and I doubt it'll be the last. But I was a bit surprised. Not a lot of deformation, considering the speed Beldock was going."

"How fast was that?" Pete asked.

"Over ninety."

Pete let out a whistle.

"Has the medical examiner made a preliminary finding?" Linda asked.

Donovan nodded. "When Beldock died, he had a blood alcohol level of point-four percent, five times Connecticut's legal intoxication limit. Have to wait for the coroner's official report. But the verdict's going to be death by misadventure. Like I said, open and shut. Especially given Beldock's history."

"Lot of cars on the road last night?" Pete asked as they headed back.

Donovan shrugged. "It was Saturday night. But it was pretty late. Not much traffic at that hour."

"Any sign of another driver?"

Donovan stopped walking and looked at Linda. "Like somebody running him off the road?"

"What about the condition of Beldock's car?" Pete asked.

"Just what you'd expect from a crash like this. Front of the car was completely demolished."

"What about the rear of the vehicle?" Linda asked.

"No damage. You really think someone was trying to kill him?" His voice rose in disbelief.

"You said Beldock was drunk," Pete quickly interjected. "Any bars near here?"

Donovan's eyes were still on Linda. "Too many. One a couple blocks away. The Red Rose Tavern. Beldock was a regular there."

"Do you know if Beldock was at the Red Rose last night?" Pete asked.

"The answer is yes. Up to his usual tricks. Trying to pick up women. But according to the bartender, he left alone." Donovan's square jaw tightened with anger. "Wife and three kids were out of town for the weekend. Family had to come home to this. You want to tell me what's going on? Something I'm missing here?"

"Don't know yet," Pete said.

But the other man wasn't ready to let it go. He knew when a fellow cop was holding out on him. "This other case you're investigating. Drunk driving accident? Or something more?"

"We're looking into it."

They'd reached their respective cars.

"Keep me in the loop, will you?" Donovan handed Pete his card.

"Sure," Pete said. "And I'd appreciate your keeping our visit on the down low."

So that the Manhattan DA's office didn't get wind of what was going on. The fatal accident had occurred less than twenty-four hours ago and in another state, so Linda hoped that Douglas Beldock's death was still under the radar.

Mike Bonaker hadn't told them about Beldock giving a statement in '84, but he said he talked to Beldock and Robbins, so their names would likely be in his police report. Which meant that Beldock and Robbins would be in the sealed record.

Donovan didn't ask any more questions, just nodded and wished them a safe drive back.

He was still standing there after Linda and Pete had gotten into their rental car and left the Hartford detective in their rearview.

59

When Linda awoke Monday morning, at first she had no idea where she was.

Then she remembered.

After leaving the scene of Douglas Beldock's fatal crash, Pete found a hotel where they could spend the night.

By that time, it was after ten. The Red Rose closed early on Sundays, so they couldn't talk to the bartender who'd served Douglas Beldock on Saturday night. After a late dinner, they checked into adjoining rooms on the third floor.

Even in her current state of anxiety combined with exhaustion, Linda had been all too aware that only a door separated her room from Pete's. She told herself that it was only natural to notice because she'd never been in a situation like this before.

Now it was almost ten o'clock in the morning—the latest she'd slept in years—and as the sun streamed in through the cheap hotel blinds, there were other things occupying her mind.

Before retiring to their respective rooms last night, she and Pete had discussed paying a visit to the body shop where Douglas Beldock's car had been taken for repairs. Just in case there was evidence that had been missed. Which happened, more often than Linda liked.

But she had no standing in Connecticut. And contacting Detective Donovan to request Beldock's widow's permission to have the car forensically examined and then asking a judge to sign off on a warrant would only direct more unwanted attention their way.

Especially after Pete found out from his contact in the NYPD that a Manhattan detective had called Mike Bonaker earlier this morning asking questions about Beldock.

As Linda had feared, the cat was out of the bag. She wouldn't be surprised if the media had also gotten wind of that and started flooding her cell with calls again.

It also meant that Detective Donovan probably knew about the case Pete had been alluding to—namely the murder of Stuart Robbins. Donovan no doubt had also received a phone call, and he might have told the Manhattan detective about Pete and Linda's visit to the Hartford PD last night.

That would explain the voicemails on Linda's phone this morning from Diane, who'd also texted. This time, she wasn't asking Linda about Guy's whereabouts or threatening her with an indictment. This was about Linda's actions. Her boss had ordered her to stay away from the Robbins case.

What Linda needed was evidence. She'd played the game long enough to know that was the only thing that would move the needle. Evidence that put Nancy Conklin in Hartford on Saturday night.

They'd start with the Red Rose Tavern, the last place Douglas Beldock was seen alive.

After a quick shower, Linda met Pete in the lobby.

"Sleep well?" he asked, managing to look well-rested and attractive despite the stubble on his chin and the fact that he was wearing the same jeans and polo shirt he'd had on yesterday.

Linda nodded. Surprisingly, she'd dropped off almost the minute her head hit the pillow. But although she'd taken a shower this morning, she felt less than fresh in her skirt and blouse she'd also put on yesterday morning.

They had a late breakfast at a coffee shop down the street, then drove the three blocks to the Red Rose Tavern.

There was only a smattering of patrons at the tavern at this hour, just after noon. Mellow jazz played from two speakers over the bar, and a TV was tuned to a local news station with the sound muted. An old-fashioned jukebox sat in the back, behind several free-standing tables.

When Linda and Pete sat down—the only two people at the bar—a red-haired kid with freckles who'd been filling small bowls with nuts and pretzels and didn't look older than eighteen immediately came over.

"What can I get you?"

Pete showed his badge. The bartender gave it a cursory glance, unfazed by the display of authority. As if police dropping into the bar was an everyday occurrence.

"Is this about the guy who crashed his car?"

Pete nodded. "Were you working Saturday night?"

"You bet. Every Saturday. Best night of the week for tips. Gotta save up to put my kids through college."

He smiled, which made him appear even younger. Linda didn't think he looked old enough to be served alcohol, let alone be a responsible father.

"You got kids?" he asked Linda.

The unexpected question blindsided her. As her hand went to her belly, for the first time, Linda was forced to consider the possibility of a future without Guy in it.

She was grateful when Pete jumped in with another question. "Did you see Douglas Beldock on Saturday night?"

The bartender nodded, his green eyes still on Linda. "He was a regular."

That jived with what Detective Donovan had told them.

"Did you serve him that night?"

The bartender shook his head and pointed down the bar, where an older man with broad shoulders, a barrel chest, and a shaved head was wiping down glasses. "Yo, Aloysius," the young bartender called. "Some people here to see you."

The man called Aloysius finished wiping and stacking a rocks glass before ambling down the bar.

"You were asking about Doug Beldock?" His voice was low and well-modulated, surprisingly soft for a man of his size.

Pete nodded. "I'm Pete. This is Linda. You served Beldock on Saturday night?"

"He sat right there." Aloysius pointed to a stool halfway down the bar. "I told that to the cop who came in yesterday."

"Detective Donovan?" Pete asked.

"Uh-huh." Aloysius leveled a glance at Pete. "You're from New York, right?"

"It's in connection with a case we're working." Pete answered his unspoken question with the pat response he'd given Donovan.

Aloysius nodded, but whether he believed Pete was another story.

"What time did Beldock get here Saturday night?"

"A little after ten. Place was packed, but Beldock found a seat at the bar. He always sat here. Easier to hit on women."

Linda placed her phone in front of him. "Do you remember seeing her here that night?"

The bartender studied the screenshot Linda had taken of Nancy Conklin's driver's license photo. "Can't say that I do."

Linda's hopes sank, even though she'd known it was a long shot. Chances were that Conklin wouldn't have wanted to risk being seen in a public place. The likelier scenario would be for her to have been lying in wait for Beldock to come out of the bar.

In the parking lot?

Which would make getting a positive ID akin to searching for the proverbial needle in a haystack.

". . . We were really busy Saturday night," Aloysius was saying. "I might have missed her." He looked over his shoulder at the freckle-faced bartender, who was hovering. "Hey, Ryan. Ever seen her before?"

Ryan glanced at the screenshot, then shook his head.

"Look again," Linda said, hating the desperation she could hear in her voice. "This woman might have been here Saturday night. Maybe at the bar."

"If you're asking if Doug Beldock hit on her, no way. She wasn't his type."

"What was his type?"

Ryan shrugged. "Young. Usually brunettes. Like the lady I saw him talking to."

"What lady?"

"The one sitting next to him."

Linda looked at Pete. Donovan hadn't mentioned that.

From the way Aloysius was looking at him, Ryan apparently hadn't told the older bartender either.

"Did you tell the detective about her?" Pete asked Ryan.

He shook his head. "Nah. I figured it was just Beldock making his usual moves. But she was really pretty. Hard not to notice her."

"This woman," Linda said. "Did she sit down next to Beldock?"

"I'm not sure. It was really crowded. Not a lot of open seats at the bar."

"Can you describe her?"

"Like I said. Brunette. Big, brown eyes. Long, dark hair."

"Do you remember who initiated the conversation?" Linda felt Pete's eyes on her, but Ryan's description of the woman had gotten her mind racing.

Ryan frowned. "I'm not sure."

"You served Beldock, right?" Linda asked Aloysius. "Did Beldock buy anyone a drink?"

Aloysius shook his head. "I only remember serving whiskey shots to Beldock. If he was talking to someone, I didn't notice, sorry. Excuse me."

He walked down the bar, where a man and woman had just sat down.

Ryan was still standing there. After a quick glance down the bar, he said, "If you're interested in the woman, I might be able to help you out." He lowered his voice to almost a conspiratorial whisper. "Like I said, she was really pretty."

"Anything else you can tell us about her?" Linda asked.

The younger bartender's eyes were still on Aloysius, who'd just handed menus to the couple. "I was serving a customer a couple seats over, and I heard Beldock telling the woman that she looked familiar and asking if they'd met before. Typical pickup line I'd heard him use on other women. She said he must be mistaken because she was new to the area. That was when Beldock introduced himself and offered to show her around. She smiled when he said that. Lord, what a pretty smile. I couldn't blame him for hitting on her. Anyways, I heard her say her name was Anna."

"No last name?"

"Nope. Just Anna."

Aloysius was coming back their way. He scowled at Ryan. "Don't you have work to do?"

After the younger bartender reluctantly headed back down the bar, Aloysius turned to Linda and Pete. "Do you mind telling me why you're asking all these questions?"

Once again, as per typical police interrogation tactics, Pete responded with a question of his own. "You told Detective Donovan that Douglas Beldock left the bar alone?"

"That's right."

"You didn't see him leave with a woman?"

"No."

But Linda heard the hesitation in his voice. And there was a troubled look on his face.

"Is there something you want to tell us?"

There was another pause before Aloysius spoke again. "When Beldock left, he was pretty drunk. Drunker than I'd ever seen him. I was worried about him driving home. It was after one by then. Place had pretty much cleared out, so I left Ryan manning the bar. In the parking lot, I saw Beldock heading to his sports car. He was weaving all over the place. Dropped his keys at one point and almost fell down trying to retrieve them. I should have grabbed them from him, called an Uber to take him home. That's something I'll regret until the day I die."

"And?"

"That was when I saw a woman. She was a brunette, but I don't know if it was the same woman Ryan saw Beldock talking to at the bar. Parking lot's not very well lit, something we're trying to work out with the city. But whoever she was, I thought she might also be concerned about Beldock. Maybe planning to offer him a lift home. But she walked in the opposite direction."

"Where was she parked?"

Aloysius gave Linda a sharp glance. "I'll show you."

Outside, in the lot behind the tavern, only a few cars were parked there. One of them was the sedan Pete had rented in the city before they set out for Manatawkett to avoid Linda's car being detected by law enforcement or the media.

"Not a lot of cars at that hour. Kind of like now." Aloysius pointed across the lot. "Beldock was parked over there on the street side. Woman was parked near the back." He indicated an area on the other side.

"Did you see who drove out of the lot first on Saturday night? Beldock or the woman?" Linda asked.

Aloysius thought for a moment. "Beldock. Took him a few minutes to start his car, though."

"Did you see the woman pull out?"

He shook his head. "I'd gone back inside by then."

"Did you happen to notice the make and model of the car she was driving?"

"Hard to say because, as I said, it's dark back there. It might have been black. Or dark blue. Compact, though. No bells and whistles."

The description of most unmarked police sedans.

Aloysius pointed to their car. "That yours?" At Pete's nod, he said, "Hers looked a lot like that."

And rental cars.

60

"It's got to be the same woman."

"We have no proof of that, Linda. No way of knowing that the woman in the parking lot was the woman sitting next to Douglas Beldock. Aloysius told us he never saw her in the bar."

"It's her. He said she was a brunette. Just like the woman outside the hotel where Stuart Robbins was killed."

"The woman you believe was Nancy Conklin's accomplice? The woman you've been so hung up on?"

They were still standing in the parking lot of the Red Rose Tavern. A few more cars had pulled in now that the lunch hour was in full swing. Linda tried to ignore the skepticism in Pete's voice as she said, "You told me yourself. The witness outside the hotel described the woman he saw as a brunette."

"He said he was pretty sure she was a brunette. He also said he only saw her from a distance. And do you know how many women fit that description?"

Linda glared at him. Was Pete being deliberately obtuse? How could he not see what was so obvious to her?

"You don't find it suspicious that she happened to sit down next to Douglas Beldock?"

"We don't know who sat down first."

"It was Beldock. She was probably waiting for a seat to open up next to him so she could make her move."

Was that how it happened with Guy? Linda wondered, not for the first time. *The woman calling herself Anna sat down next to him at a bar?*

"Linda, do you hear yourself? This is all assumption. Not one piece of real evidence. You'd be laughed out of a courtroom. The case would never even make it to trial. Which you'd know if you weren't so close to this."

"I know what you're thinking, and you're wrong. This isn't about Guy."

"Isn't it? And there's also—"

"Also what?"

"You're having a baby."

"So it's hormones now. This is a female thing, right? I can't be trusted to use my brain because my emotions are making me irrational?"

"You know me better than that. I'm more of a feminist than most of the women I work with. That's not what I'm saying."

"Then what are you saying?"

"Okay." Pete held up a hand in a peace offering. "Let's say, for argument's sake, it's the same woman. That means she's the one who ran Beldock off the road."

"Right."

"So she isn't an accomplice, but a killer?"

"Hired by Nancy Conklin. Don't look at me like that. It's not as if the animal doesn't exist. Do you know that more than fifty percent of assassins today are female?"

"So she killed Stuart Robbins?"

"Why not? There's no evidence that Nancy Conklin murdered Robbins."

"And there's no evidence that this woman ran Douglas Beldock off the road."

"So far. Listen to me, Pete. Please. Call it hormones. Feminine intuition. Whatever you want. But I know I'm right about this. Now are you going to help me or not?"

"You know the answer to that."

"Good. Now we just need to find her."

"How do you propose we do that?"

Linda watched as more cars pulled into the lot. "I've been thinking about this. From Aloysius's description, it sounded like she might have been driving a rental car. Maybe she rented it from a place around here."

"Why would she rent a car that would leave a paper trail? She'd have to give ID."

"Which would be as phony as she is. How many criminals did you arrest who were carrying fraudulent IDs? She uses fake creds to rent a car. Returns the car after she no longer needs it. And no one's the wiser."

She had her phone out and was already Googling car rental companies in the Hartford area.

"Linda—"

"Humor me, okay?"

61

Linda's search had turned up the names of the three well-known car rental companies with addresses in cities all across the country. All located in town, within a few minutes' drive of each other.

Gaining access to the drivers' licenses of people who'd rented cars in the last few days wasn't hard. All Pete had to do was flash his badge, and the companies were only too happy to oblige. The last thing any of them wanted was negative publicity, especially after Pete told them he was investigating a suspicious death that might have involved a rental car.

But none of the drivers' license photos Linda and Pete sifted through at the three companies bore the slightest resemblance to the woman Ryan had described.

They had just parked across the street from a car rental place a few miles outside Hartford that Linda found after she extended the search. She hoped that the fourth time would be the charm.

Inside, the middle-aged woman at the front desk with tendrils of blond-gray hair escaping a loose bun looked harried. Probably due to the documents strewn haphazardly across the desk. No doubt catching up on paperwork.

After Pete shared his credentials, the woman's blue eyes widened in alarm. She told him that she was Joan Frank, the owner, and asked if something was wrong.

For the fourth time that day, Pete explained he was investigating a suspicious death that might have involved a rental car.

The woman grew even more agitated. In answer to Pete's question, Joan Frank said that they'd rented only a handful of cars over the weekend. Two on Saturday afternoon. Which fit the parameters of the timeline between Stuart Robbins's murder Friday night and Douglas Beldock's death late Saturday night—technically Sunday morning.

The first customer was a middle-aged male who'd rented a luxury sedan.

The second was a woman who'd rented a midnight-blue compact sedan.

Even in the grainy photo, Linda could see that the woman smiling for the DMV camera was gorgeous. With long, dark hair, just as Ryan had described. Down to her big, brown eyes.

The address on the license listed a street in Pikesville, Maryland. Which might or might not exist. Not that that mattered if the rest of the license was fake.

Linda skimmed over the date of birth—1985—and other identifying facts, such as the description of her brown hair and brown eyes, which she already knew.

The first name on the license wasn't Anna, as Linda had known it wouldn't be.

It was Hunter.

Hunter Rellim.

No doubt another alias.

The last name was a new one to Linda. One that she hadn't heard before. Maybe because it was pure invention on the part of Hunter, or whoever she really was.

Although when she Googled the name, Linda found that a person with the same name actually existed. But she didn't live at the Maryland address that was on the driver's license. Nor did the young girl with the curly, blond hair smiling out from her Instagram profile fit the description of the woman Linda was looking for.

According to Joan Frank, the rental car hadn't been returned yet. That wasn't unusual, given that the place was closed on Sunday. They often had a run on returned cars on Monday and Tuesday.

Which meant that Anna/Hunter could still be in the area.

But why, if she'd accomplished what she set out to do? More likely, she'd already ditched the car and was off the radar. Which left them back at square one.

Linda tried to shake off her growing frustration. This was their first real lead—the evidence sat on the desk right in front of her—but she had no idea how to find their elusive quarry who seemed to always be one step ahead of them.

While Pete talked to Joan Frank, Linda picked up the driver's license again. Something drew her gaze back to the name under the photo. Was it just wishful thinking?

Or had she heard the name somewhere before?

62

With two of them dead, that left one.

Douglas Beldock's death was a shock, something Bonaker hadn't expected. Yet it made perfect sense.

Guy Kingship must have read about Dorothy Miller's suicide dredging up the old crime, and it spooked him. He wasn't taking any chances and was now picking off the other two to make sure there were no witnesses. So that Robbins and Beldock couldn't turn on Kingship in order to secure a deal for themselves.

That would be the obvious play. Robbins and Beldock would want to avoid the possibility of being arrested as accomplices, which carried the same charge as murder. Even if Kingship wasn't married to a lawyer, he might know that there was no statute of limitations on the ultimate crime.

Linda Haley Kingship knew that too. Bonaker had seen her reaction when he brought it up. She'd figured out he had something.

Bonaker had wondered what else she knew, tried to call her bluff to get her to give up Kingship. She'd obviously come to Manatawkett to gather ammunition for his defense.

She seemed to believe in his innocence. Bonaker had to give her that. But he'd bet his eyeteeth that Kingship hadn't told her what happened in '84.

That he'd killed before.

And might have been part of the gang rape of a defenseless woman. Those weren't things that a man wanted to share with his wife.

If Bonaker had had evidence that Kingship and his friends assaulted Dorothy Miller back in '84, they would have all gone to prison for that crime alone.

He couldn't get Kingship for the rape now. Although there'd been no statute of limitions on rape since 2006, the clock had tolled on the long-ago assault.

But if it turned out that Douglas Beldock's death hadn't been an accident, a third murder could be added to the crimes against Guy Kingship.

And this time, Bonaker was going to make sure the charges stuck.

Kingship's DNA on the torn chain could be the final nail in his coffin and could put him in prison for the rest of his natural life.

That's what Bonaker was banking on. DNA wouldn't be any use to him if it turned out to belong to Robbins or Beldock. They couldn't be prosecuted from beyond the grave.

He hadn't shared that piece of evidence with the NYPD detective who'd called to drop the bombshell about Beldock ten minutes after Bonaker walked into his office Monday morning. And to ask if Bonaker would be willing to provide more details about his questioning of Douglas Beldock in connection with the '84 murder of Alfred Johnson.

Bonaker said he was glad to be of assistance but that he stood by what was in his original report. Beldock had refused to answer questions and was never a suspect in the Johnson murder. The detective thanked him for his time and asked Bonaker to reach out if he remembered anything from the old case.

The detective didn't ask about the assault on Dorothy Miller that Bonaker had also written up in his report because that crime was never proven, and no one could be charged with it now. But the assault could provide the motive for Alfred Johnson's murder.

Before he ended the call, Bonaker asked if there was any progress in the search for Guy Kingship. He was told that the search was ongoing.

Bonaker hadn't seen the use in bringing Alfred Johnson's torn chain to the attention of the NYPD when he still didn't know if the Riverhead lab could recover DNA. He wasn't a big believer in God or fate or whatever you wanted to call it, especially after Ruby died such an agonizing, drawn-out death. But he had to believe that the torn chain had come into his possession for a reason.

Yet even if DNA were found, Bonaker still needed Kingship for a match.

He just had to hope that sooner or later, Kingship would slip up.

Make a mistake.

Like all criminals.

He couldn't stay off the grid forever.

63

"... I wasn't the one who rented her the car. That was Jonathan. My husband." Joan Frank's tone was defensive as she tried to explain herself to Pete. "I'm not passing the buck. Jonathan and I are joint owners in the business. But something like this has never happened to us before."

Linda listened with only half an ear as she continued to study Hunter Rellim's driver's license to figure out why that first name jumped out at her.

"... As you can see, we're a small, family-owned company. Competing with the big three. Not that we cut corners, and we'd never willingly be part of anything criminal. We still have a reputation to uphold."

Frank's next words caught Linda's attention.

"... couldn't blame him. Jonathan has a weakness for pretty women. I was working on another rental agreement when she came in, but I noticed her right away. She really was beautiful. The kind of looks that could drive men crazy. I'm not saying that I don't trust my husband."

When a girl is as beautiful as Dorothy was, women are bound to be suspicious. Don't trust them. And don't trust their men around them.

Jesse Edwards had described Dorothy Miller in almost the exact same words.

Then Linda remembered Ryan saying he overheard Douglas Beldock telling the woman who'd sat down next to him in the bar that she looked familiar and asking if they'd met before.

Ryan thought it was a pickup line.

Not a pickup line.

Not this time.

Linda closed her eyes and pictured the shrine in Nancy Conklin's backyard.

The framed photo of Dorothy Miller on the beach in Manatawkett, smiling into the camera with the ocean behind her.

Miller's hair was dark red. And her eyes were blue.

The woman in the driver's license photo had brown hair and brown eyes.

But that smile.

How could she have missed what had been in plain sight from the beginning?

She'd been right all along. This was about revenge. She just had the wrong person.

Linda wasn't aware she'd gotten up until she was standing next to Pete.

"What was her name?"

Pete and the rental car owner looked at her.

"Whose name?" Pete asked.

"Mike Bonaker told us, don't you remem—"

It was Hunter.

That was why the name on the driver's license had struck a chord.

Not a first name.

A last.

She must have gotten married after she left Manatawkett.

Linda turned a dazed face to Pete.

"We need to find out."

"Find out what?"

"If Dorothy Miller had a child."

PART III

64

The sound blasted his eardrums and drove into his skull.

When he opened his eyes, his face was pressed into the unyielding leather of the steering wheel.

Guy lifted his head.

The noise abruptly stopped, but he could still hear the horn's reverberation, pounding in sync with the drumbeat in his brain. He felt the different parts of his body rebelling as he tried to ease himself into a more upright position. His right arm was numb from having been in one position for too long, trapped between his body and the wheel.

Cool air was coming in through the driver's side open window. Guy turned, the crick in his neck making the movement painful.

All he saw was darkness. He glanced at the clock on the dashboard. Seven twenty-five.

In the morning? Evening?

When did he park here? Wherever "here" was.

He squinted, which sent a thousand needles stabbing into his eyelids, careful to crane his neck slowly to gaze outside. Just the same pervasive darkness. Except for the pale rays of sun he could now see slanting in through the tops of trees.

Trees?

On the breeze, he could hear it. The rustling of leaves.

As his eyes grew accustomed to the dimness, he sensed movement. Saw the bushy tail of a squirrel as it scampered up the trunk of a tree. Heard the hoot of an owl perched on a high branch.

In the distance, he could make out the old, weathered sign for a campground that had closed years ago.

He knew these woods. They were a part of the reserve that abutted his backyard. The defunct campground was less than a mile from his house.

He had a flash of being behind the wheel as he turned a corner. It had been dark out, no moon or even a single star in the sky as he turned onto his block.

Had he been driving home from the train station? What happened after that? How did he end up here, sleeping in his car? Did he and Linda have a fight?

Why couldn't he remember?

He saw himself sitting at a bar, a shot glass in front of him.

Guy closed his eyes to bring back the memory, but his mind remained maddeningly blank. His mouth felt as parched as the desert. He turned and reached into the netted compartment in the back for one of the water bottles he always kept there. After guzzling it down, he wiped his mouth and caught sight of himself in the rearview mirror.

There was an ugly gash on his forehead.

He watched his reflection as his fingers gingerly probed the wound. It felt raw and tender.

He slipped his fingers beneath his hairline, and they came away sticky with dried blood.

In his mind's eye, he saw a room filled with shadows, the only unnatural illumination coming from the generic, hotel-grade lamps.

One of those lamps, the shade covered in blood, lay on its side on the cheap hardwood floor.

That's when things came rushing back in one giant, vertiginous wave.

Tossing down shots in a bar while waiting for Anna. Worried that something had happened to her.

Getting into a fight with someone.

Being asked to leave.

After that, all he remembered was waking up in a hotel room. The shock of realizing he was alone with a dead body, Anna nowhere to be seen.

Hearing voices through the room's thin walls.

Creeping into the dingy, dimly lit hallway. The voices louder here. Seeing the pair of them as Guy crouched on the top step.

In the lobby talking to a pimply kid behind the desk.

Cops.

Looking frantically around for a way out. Remembering the fire escape he'd seen through the window at the end of the hall. The voices getting louder as he struggled to open the window, which was caked with grime.

Making it outside as he heard the cops moving toward the stairs.

Jumping down from the fire escape, winded but not hurt after landing on the grass.

Leaping to his feet. Expecting to hear the sound of sirens as he ran across and down city blocks.

Racing down the steps of the subway.

Catching the last train out of Grand Central. Few commuters at that hour, but feeling as if every last one of them was staring at him.

It wasn't until he was driving home that he realized his phone was missing.

He remembered looking at the clock on the dashboard, thinking that Linda would have been home for hours by now. She would have wondered where he was. Called or texted him.

The phone wasn't in its usual place in the right pocket of his jacket.

Or the left.

Had he lost his phone when he fled the hotel? If he had, the police would likely have it by now.

Or he could have lost it on the subway.

The train?

The hotel room? That would be even worse.

He checked his jacket pockets again. The phone wasn't there.

He checked the floor mats and under the seats. No phone.

He had a flash of turning onto his block and continuing past his house.

Now he knew why. If he had lost his phone in the hotel room, Linda was bound to find out. If she didn't already know.

She worked for the Manhattan DA's office. If he told her what happened, which he wasn't sure he knew, she'd have a real conflict of interest. She might feel compelled to tell the police his whereabouts.

His head began to throb, and he felt the crown of his head. A sizable lump had formed.

He once again saw himself in the hotel room. The lamp on its side on the floor, its shade covered in blood. Remembering now seeing the lamp cord next to the body.

Clear signs of a struggle.

Between him and the dead man? Was that how he ended up with the injury to his head?

What about Anna? Where was she? Was she okay?

And if Linda didn't know, she had to be worried sick by now.

Guy pounded the wheel in frustration. Then he turned on the radio. It was set to his favorite classical station. He switched to the local news, but all he heard was static.

His hand shook as he slid the key into his pocket. He glanced out the window, but there wasn't a person in sight. He realized that must have been why he'd chosen this particular spot, knowing it would be free of human traffic.

He fought the urge to stay where he was, even though he knew it was only a matter of time before the police found him.

Again, he thought about his wife. What must be going through Linda's head right now?

His hand shook as he reached into the glove compartment. He had to know what happened in that hotel room. Before he lost his mind completely.

65

H er name was Samantha Hunter.

She lived in Pikesville, Maryland. That part of the address on her phony driver's license was real.

It was the street address that didn't exist.

The lane where Samantha Hunter actually resided was around the corner from the house where her mother had lived for thirty-eight years with her husband, Richard Hunter.

Pete was the one who figured out why she'd chosen Rellim as a last name.

While it was true that Linda had found a woman with the same name on Facebook, in this case, Rellim wasn't a real name. It was an anagram.

Miller spelled backwards.

All of which Linda told Diane when she returned her calls while pacing the length of the tiny parking lot of the Frank & Frank car rental company.

Night had fallen and the lot wasn't well lit, but Linda barely noticed. She'd come out here because she needed to get some air. Pete was still inside talking to Joan Frank's husband, Jonathan, who'd arrived a short while ago.

Her boss was quiet for a long time after Linda had finished. When Diane finally spoke, her words came out on a sigh. "I'm sorry, Linda. But so far, all I've heard is theory and supposition."

Because Samantha Hunter had covered her tracks well.

She had to have been planning this for months.

"She's Dorothy Miller's daughter. Two of the men who raped her mother are dead. That's motive right there. In spades." Linda was desperate to make Diane understand. "She presented fake ID to rent a car that she planned to use as a murder weapon. What more do you need?"

"Facts, Linda. Which you'd be questioning if you weren't blinded by your need to prove your husband's innocence. You know as well as I do that right now there isn't one solid piece of evidence linking Samantha Hunter to the deaths of Stuart Robbins and Douglas Beldock. The only evidence in the hotel room where Robbins was found belongs to Guy."

"Because Hunter lured him there."

"You have proof of that?"

The woman a witness had seen outside the Manhattan hotel. But Linda refrained from mentioning that, remembering how skeptical Pete had been. Although he'd since apologized for doubting her.

Small comfort now.

Diane was still talking. "If we find Hunter, we could have her arrested for possession of a forged instrument. That's fraud and a felony, as you know. But it doesn't make her a murderer. Even if witnesses at the Red Rose Tavern saw Hunter talking to Douglas Beldock on Saturday night, it doesn't put her at the scene. We have no witnesses who saw her following him in her car. And according to Detective Donovan of the Hartford PD, there's no proof that Beldock's death was anything other than an accident."

"What did Mike Bonaker tell you when you called him?"

Diane's hesitation told Linda that she was deciding the best way to play this and at the same time gather information. Her usual MO.

"We're not hiding anything, Linda. Just doing a thorough investigation. None of which is new to you.'

"You never told me about the sealed record."

"I was under no obligation to do that, and you know it. And I told you to stay away from the investigation."

"If I'd listened to you, I wouldn't have found Samantha Hunter."

"Point taken." Diane's tone softened. "In answer to your question, we wanted to know what Bonaker could tell us about the murder of Alfred Johnson."

"To build your case against Guy for Stuart Robbins. Guy didn't kill anyone," Linda said into the silence that had fallen.

"Guy was the one arrested in '84," Diane said.

As if Linda needed reminding. "The charges were dropped."

"Mike Bonaker also told us that he never had definitive evidence of an assault on Dorothy Miller. Even if Miller was raped and Samantha Hunter has embarked on some kind of revenge crusade, until we have enough for probable cause, my hands are tied."

Which meant they couldn't get a subpoena to access Hunter's cell phone records. Or a warrant to search her house.

Not that they'd find her.

And a woman cunning enough to have orchestrated two fiendish crimes wouldn't make the mistake of leaving her cell phone on.

"I'm sorry, Linda," Diane said.

"Did Bonaker tell you he had new evidence?"

"What evidence are you talking about?"

So Bonaker hadn't told the DA's office. Why not?

Did the evidence implicate Guy in Alfred Johnson's murder? Or had the Manatawkett police chief been bluffing, after all?

The door of the rental company opened, and Pete walked out. Even in the dim light, she could tell instantly that something was up.

"I have to go, Diane."

"Linda, if you know something—"

But Linda had ended the call. "What?" she asked as Pete approached her.

"Let's go. I'll tell you on the way."

"On the way where?" She had to hurry to keep up with him.

Pete didn't answer until they were inside their car and he was backing out of the lot. "We've located Samantha Hunter's rental car."

"How?"

"That's what I was talking to Jonathan Frank about. A lot of car rental companies install GPS trackers in their vehicles because of the high incidence of theft. Mostly in luxury sedans. Turns out, there's a tracking device in the compact they rented to Samantha Hunter. All they had to do was activate it."

"So she ditched the rental. Maybe she hasn't gotten that far yet. Where is it? Pete?"

"A parking lot in Scarsdale."

For a second, Linda could swear her heart stopped beating.

That made no sense.

Unless—

Did Hunter know something that Linda didn't?

Had Guy come home?

Why?

He'd gotten tired of running?

"Hunter drove to Scarsdale for a reason," Pete said as they headed for the exit to the highway. "She wouldn't risk exposure otherwise."

"It isn't over." Linda could barely get out the words.

Because her plan had failed.

Guy was still free.

And out there somewhere.

She wasn't going to stop. Not when she'd already killed twice.

They had to find Guy before Samantha Hunter did.

66

That was a narrow escape.

He'd been arguing with himself during the entire walk into town. Kept looking over his shoulder, any minute expecting to see cops converging on his car.

All Guy saw was the shiny chrome of his SUV winking through the trees.

The wooded trail that wound through Scarsdale and the neighboring towns was one he'd trekked often in the past. Back when he was writing a novel and used to take solitary hikes to clear his head and hear himself think.

In another lifetime.

He wasn't sure how long he'd been walking when the trail ended abruptly in a dirt path that eventually turned into the paved streets of the town.

Once on Main Street, a ubiquitous place in every town in America, he pulled the brim of the baseball cap lower. As he crossed the busy intersection, he was hit by the same unsettling feeling he'd experienced earlier as he took the cap out of the glove compartment, along with his extra pair of sunglasses.

Not that he thought it made a whit of difference, especially now that it was dark out and he didn't need the shades. Sunglasses and low-billed caps were what most criminals wore to conceal their identity, which only made them stick out like sore thumbs.

Inside the 7-Eleven, he felt even more exposed.

The teenager at the checkout line barely gave him a glance as she rang up his items. He handed her a couple of bills, then immediately slid the wallet containing his photo ID back into his pocket. As she handed him his change, he wondered what he was going to do when he ran out of cash.

Guy was leaving the store when he saw the police car pull up.

His heart rate spiking, he fell into step behind another exiting customer. He walked as slowly as he could, picking up speed as he continued down the block.

It was only after he'd crossed the intersection and was on the other side of the street that he dared to turn around.

The patrol car was still double-parked in front of the 7-Eleven, but the cop was no longer at the wheel. He'd gone into the store.

That was when Guy started running.

After he was safely back in the woods, weak-kneed with relief that he'd gotten away, he realized that he was starting to think like a criminal.

And act like one.

He put the sunglasses and baseball cap back in the glove compartment, and stood in front of the car, pulling out the newspaper he had tucked under his arm.

Unfolding the paper, he laid it on the top of the car. Then he took out the flashlight he'd bought at the 7-Eleven, flipped it on, and opened the paper to the Metro section.

It was the third article from the top on the first page.

SUSPECT STILL BEING SOUGHT IN
FRIDAY NIGHT MURDER IN
LOWER MANHATTAN HOTEL

Police are searching for the man believed to have brutally murdered another man Friday night in a room at the Moonrise Hotel on Hudson Street, an area long known for prostitution.

His heart nearly stopped when he saw his name.
The name he'd once envisioned gracing the cover of a novel.

. . . Guy Kingship is the husband of Linda Haley, a prosecutor with the Manhattan District Attorney's office.

Linda.
Guilt again reached out its tentacles.
What could she be thinking?
He again felt the urge to call his wife, if only to hear her voice. But what words of comfort could Linda give? And he couldn't put her in that position, make her have to choose between her job and him.
And if he did speak to her, what would he say?
I'm sorry, Linda.

For what?

Everything?

Guy forced himself to keep reading.

A member of the NYPD, who spoke on condition of ano-
nymity, told this newspaper that the police have evidence in
their possession that places Kingship in the hotel room . . .

It had to be his phone. That was how they zeroed in on him so quickly.

. . . also have physical evidence . . .

Physical evidence?

. . . Fingerprints found on the outside of the door of the hotel
room and the inside doorknob . . .

He had a sudden memory of reaching out his hand. Watching the door swing open.

Then waking up on the floor of the hotel room. Realizing he must have been drunker than he thought and wondering how long he'd been passed out.

When he ran out of the room, had he also left his fingerprints on the doorknob?

Police are searching for a connection between Kingship and
the victim, whose name has just been released.

According to documents found in the room, the dead man is believed to be Stuart Robbins . . .

Guy could swear his heart stopped beating altogether.

It had to be a mistake. A misprint.

Someone else who happened to have that name.

What were the odds that it was the same Stuart Robbins?

He flashed again to the hotel room.

Now that he thought about it, hadn't there been something vaguely familiar about the body next to the bed, despite the additional pounds and almost completely bald head poking through the blood matting the dead man's skull?

He'd just remembered something else, from before he woke up in the room.

Sneaking into the hotel and up the stairs to the room where Anna was hiding out from her abusive boyfriend.

Once again, Guy saw himself standing in front of a closed door. Just like in his recurring dream.

Had he gone into the wrong room? A room containing the corpse of someone he knew? What were the odds of that happening?

Assuming that Robbins was dead when he got there. The condition of the room—the lamp on the floor—and the lump on Guy's head showed clear evidence of a struggle.

A thought hit him that chilled him to the core.

Had he killed Stuart Robbins, then passed out and woken up with no memory of what happened?

Why would he kill him in the first place? He hadn't laid eyes on Robbins in almost four decades.

Not since that terrible summer.

When someone else died.

Alfred Johnson.

He never forgot his name.

There was a lot he hadn't forgotten.

The strange thing was, he thought he'd been dreaming about that summer in Manatawkett when he woke up in the car.

Dreaming about Dorothy.

The girl he'd loved.

And lost.

Guy never saw Dorothy again after he left Manatawkett.

Never knew what happened to her.

She was part of that time in his life that he'd put in a lockbox and then buried the key. That was the only way he could go on living with himself after his mother took her life at the end of August.

His father's drinking became worse after she died. Louis Kingship blamed his son for her suicide, saying that Rachel Kingship couldn't live with the shame and disgrace of what happened in Manatawkett. That he should have left Guy to rot in prison.

It took a supreme effort of will to drag his mind out of the black hole of the past.

Guy reread the article about Stuart Robbins, hoping to find something that would help him make sense of all this.

Below the article was a teaser for a related piece. He found it a few pages later.

Nothing about the murder, just a few paragraphs about other crimes that had taken place at the hotel over the years.

Guy was about to close the paper when a squib at the bottom of the page caught his eye.

It was another name he recognized.

A sense of unreality swept over Guy as he read the obituary about the son of an international banking CEO.

Then read it a second time.

On the next page were the details of how he died.

Douglas Beldock's car went off the road Saturday night.

Beldock and Stuart Robbins had been inseparable in high school.

Now they were both dead.

What the hell was going on?

Guy looked at the date at the top of the page.

Monday.

His hand trembled as he flipped back through the pages.

Stuart Robbins was killed Friday night.

Douglas Beldock died in a drunk driving accident late Saturday night.

The chill turned to ice water in his veins.

Guy had no memory of where he'd been or what he'd been doing between driving past his house Friday night and waking up in his car a few hours ago.

Just like that August night forty years ago when he had that confrontation with Alfred Johnson outside the abandoned lighthouse.

The next thing he remembered was standing next to the railing on the lighthouse roof, his jaw throbbing and his right eye swollen shut, looking down through the haze of his blurred vision and seeing Johnson's body floating in the ocean.

Like waking up in a hotel room with a dead body.

History repeating itself? Down to the drunken blackout and a head injury attesting to some kind of a fight?

All these years later, even after being arrested and the charges being dropped, he was no closer to knowing if he killed Alfred Johnson.

Had his father been right about him after all?

All he knew now was the three boys from that long-ago summer were dead.

That was when Guy started to shake.

He was shaking so hard he didn't hear it at first.

Footsteps in the underbrush.

It had to be the cop he'd seen going into the 7-Eleven. He must have followed him back to the woods.

Then he heard a familiar voice.

"Hello, Guy."

67

S lowly, he turned around.

Dorothy was standing there.

Her hair tumbled down around her shoulders. Thick and wavy, just the way Guy remembered.

But it was the wrong color. Not dark red. Dark brown. Almost black. And her eyes weren't dark blue. They were brown.

"We meet again."

Her voice was different too.

Guy blinked, then his vision cleared.

It wasn't Dorothy.

But the woman standing in front of him wasn't anyone Guy had ever seen before. Not with her lovely face a mask of rage.

"Anna?" His voice rose in disbelief.

"That's not my name."

"I don't understand. Who are you?"

"You really don't know? Douglas Beldock had no idea who I was either. You know what he asked me in the bar? If we'd met before. That

I looked familiar. He kept staring at me, trying to figure out where he knew me from. After a few shots, he said maybe it was because I reminded him of a girl he once knew. My mother was just some girl he and his friends raped."

Guy felt as if he'd been sucker punched.

Dorothy had a daughter?

"But Beldock knew who I was when I followed him down that dark country road. So drunk he could hardly stay in his lane. I smiled at him as I passed. Saw the recognition finally dawn. His eyes practically bugging out of his head as he sped up to get away. But I was too fast. Then I saw the tree coming up. I was right behind him when he lost control of the wheel."

Her eyes blazed with fury.

"I didn't remind Stuart Robbins of anyone. He could barely keep his hands to himself when I took his order at a Manhattan men's club filled with predators smoking cigars and bragging about their conquests. I was already there when Robbins walked into the hotel room I'd told him to reserve that night. The perfect off-the-beaten-path place for a married man to be anonymous. I made sure he also knew who I was before I killed him. He tried to worm his way out of it. Said he never touched her. Liar! Did you know he was arrested for sexual assault three times, and each time the charges were dropped? Which brings us to you."

Her tone had become almost conversational. She could have been talking about the weather.

"I watched you reading on the train. All I had to do was wait until there was an open seat next to you. The rest was easy. I'd read about your mother's suicide along with the rumors about your father's abuse. Pretending to be a victim was the perfect way to lure you to the hotel."

She shook her head. "You should have been in prison by now. After I left you in the hotel, I made an anonymous call to nine-one-one. But you got away."

"You were in the room?" Then he answered his own question. "You hit me with the lamp."

Guy remembered that now. He hadn't passed out from the Scotch. He saw himself waking up in his car, his fingers coming away from his forehead sticky with blood.

It had all been part of her plan.

And he'd fallen for it.

"You were so easy to seduce. Because you're all the same."

"No."

But he'd met her, hadn't he?

It was he who'd asked to join her for drinks that first night. And then went on to meet her again and again. Even before she fed him what had obviously been a fictional story about being abused by the man she was living with.

Because he subliminally knew who she was?

Hadn't he recognized her from the moment she appeared on the train and asked if the seat next to him was taken?

"My mother was nothing to you. To any of you. A nobody you forgot after you raped her. And she would have stayed forgotten if she hadn't gone back to Manatawkett."

"You're wrong. I—" Guy stopped. "Dorothy went back to Manatawkett?"

She nodded. But something had changed in her face.

"When?"

"Six months ago."

"Why did she go back?"

"To die."

Dorothy was dead?

"How did she—"

"She jumped off the lighthouse roof."

As if it were yesterday, Guy saw himself on the roof of the abandoned lighthouse with Dorothy.

"You're standing too close to the edge. Those railings aren't safe."

"How many feet up do you think we are?"

"A lot. A hundred and eleven, if you really want to know. Please, D. Come back."

Dorothy pointed at the observation tower. "You must have heard the stories about the lighthouse keeper who hanged himself. As a kid, I always wondered. Why didn't he just jump? After he went under the waves, he might have floated away with the tide. Maybe his body would never have been found and he'd end up lying with the fishes, safe in the sea forever."

Guy felt Dorothy's daughter's eyes on him as he struggled to control his emotions.

He couldn't believe that Dorothy was dead. He felt the finality of her death like a physical blow.

"Enough talk."

Guy could hear it in her voice. She'd come here to kill him.

Just like she'd killed Stuart Robbins and Douglas Beldock.

Guy looked around the deserted woods.

No sound but the occasional birdcall and chittering of small forest animals. He turned back to her. "How did you know where to find me?"

She cocked her head in that way he'd always found impossible to resist and gave him a knowing smile as she opened her hand.

In her palm was a cell phone. She scrolled across the screen. When she held up the phone, Guy could see a white square app with the word "tile" in the middle.

"All I had to do was drop the tracker in your car when you offered me a lift home from the train station. It was so small you wouldn't have noticed it."

That was the night they shared their first drink. When they toasted to having met on the train.

"You thought of everything, didn't you?"

She shook her head as she turned off the phone, then slid it into her pocket. "You weren't supposed to die. Just be arrested and spend the rest of your life in prison. The way you should have been when you killed the boyfriend of my mother's best friend. You got away with it then. I was going to make sure you didn't get away this time."

"I didn't—"

"Didn't what? Kill Alfred Johnson?"

"I . . . I can't remember."

She stared at him in disbelief. "You don't remember pushing him off of the roof?"

Guy shook his head. "I don't remember much about that night." To his everlasting shame and regret. "Except—I know I was meeting Dorothy. We made plans."

"That's a lie."

"It's the truth. I swear."

"You can tell yourself that all you like. It won't change what you did."

Guy stared at her in horror. "Did Dorothy tell you I raped her?"

"She didn't tell me anything."

"Then how do you know?"

When she didn't answer, his mind started to race.

Who could have told her? Nancy Conklin?

He'd always suspected that Conklin knew about his relationship with Dorothy. But how did Conklin know what happened at the abandoned lighthouse that night? She wasn't there.

Or was she?

Had she been spying on them? Looking for Alfred Johnson? Or had Dorothy told her?

A memory rose up.

He was back in the city two weeks after his father had gotten the murder charge dropped and they'd driven home, his mother stiff and unsmiling in the front seat.

Desperate to talk to Dorothy, Guy walked to a pay phone a few blocks from their apartment building and called Nancy Conklin.

Conklin told him Dorothy had left town. Then she started screaming that it was all his fault and he only got off because his father was a judge. That he and his friends thought they were better than the rest of them, and they'd be punished for ruining good people's lives by taking what didn't belong to them.

Then she hung up.

Dorothy's daughter was studying him. "It doesn't matter how I found out. You know what you did. I can see it in your eyes."

"No. I . . . I can't remember." Guy once again tried to dredge it up, but as always, he hit an impenetrable wall. His last memory before the Manatawkett cop showed up on the lighthouse roof was standing at the railing, staring down at Alfred Johnson's body in the water.

"How do you know you didn't do it if you can't remember?"

She'd just articulated the fear that had shadowed him most of his life.

"I loved Dorothy." Guy heard his voice crack, was swamped by an overwhelming feeling of loss.

"I don't believe you."

"It's true."

She didn't say anything but moved so fast that he never saw her reach into her bag.

There was a gun in her hand.

Guy forced his gaze back up to her face. He saw the implacable set to her jaw. "Don't do this."

"You're just trying to save yourself."

"Even if you don't believe me. Don't make Dorothy's death mean nothing. Don't destroy your life too."

"It's too late."

There was something in her voice. As if she already knew the end and was resigned to her fate. The realization chilled him. After she shot him, was she planning to kill herself?

The way her mother had?

And his mother?

"Anna, please." Guy didn't know what else to call her. "I won't tell anyone. No one will know you were here. You can still walk away."

The way he'd watched her do so many times before, vanishing into the rush-hour crowds in Grand Central, as if she'd never been there.

She shook her head.

"What are you going to do? Shoot me and bury my body in the woods?"

Less than a mile from his house.

"You're the writer. You tell me how this story ends."

She pointed the gun at him.

"Start walking."

68

"**C**an't you drive any faster?"

"Not unless you want us to get stopped for speeding," Pete said. "Then we'll end up losing more time."

Time was what they didn't have.

Linda tried to tamp down the panic that had ratcheted up her heart rate and was twisting her stomach into knots. She felt a pang that could have been a contraction. Closing her eyes, she forced herself to breathe.

It was approximately a ninety-minute drive from Hartford to Scarsdale.

Now it was after ten. They'd been on the road an hour.

All Linda's calls to their landline at home had been picked up by the voicemail message she'd recorded years ago.

A search of their house by NYPD detectives had revealed no sign of Guy or evidence of forced entry to indicate that an abduction had taken place. There was no evidence that Guy ever came home at all.

Detectives found Samantha Hunter's car in a long-term lot near the Scarsdale shopping center where Linda had often parked back when she lived the approximation of a normal domestic existence.

The car was in the precise location where the GPS tracking device had led law enforcement. It was abandoned, which came as no surprise to anyone.

Twenty minutes ago, the search had been extended to the woods that ran through Scarsdale and where Linda used to go jogging along a trail near a long-abandoned campground.

The woods were part of a reserve that bordered the rear of the Kingship property.

The campground was less than a mile from their house.

If Guy had returned to the area and been taken, the woods offered the best concealment.

The perfect place to commit murder and dispose of a body.

Linda's phone was still in her hand when it buzzed. Her boss's face came up on the tiny screen. Linda's hand shook as she accepted the call.

Diane's voice filled the cabin.

"They found Guy's car."

69

He'd hardly ever been here this late at night.

And only on rare occasions, usually as a result of inclement weather, had Guy waited inside the neo-Tudor house, with its Spanish tiled green roof that made it look like a home in some exotic locale.

Now its windows were dark. The only light emanated from the tall lamps at either end, illuminating the name SCARSDALE printed in black letters on a rectangular sign affixed to the railing above the platform. Without its usual crush of commuters, the station had a spectral, haunted aspect.

Which was fitting, in a way.

Guy looked at the woman standing a few feet from him, in almost the exact spot where he'd once told her to wait on line in order to get the best seat on the train.

She was a ghost.

From his past.

The daughter of the girl he'd loved. Only the gun pointed at his heart reminded him that she was also a killer.

"You won't get away with it."

She laughed; a harsh, mirthless sound that Guy had never heard from her before. Her beautiful face was devoid of expression, the occasional flash of her brown eyes revealing the rage beneath the surface.

"Of course I'll get away with it. And this will work out even better."

"How?" There was still a part of Guy that couldn't believe she'd murdered in cold blood. "You can't kill three people without leaving a trail. It's only a matter of time before you're caught."

"How will I get caught when no one's looking for me? That's the beauty of my plan. Who's going to connect the three deaths to a forty-year-old unsolved murder? Or even to each other?"

She tossed back her long, dark hair, revealing her elegant, swan-like neck.

"The police think you killed Stuart Robbins because the two of you were fighting over a hooker. Douglas Beldock was drunk and crashed into a tree. And if by some remote chance they connected the three of you to that night at the lighthouse, they'll think you ran Beldock off the road. Either way, you couldn't live with what you'd done. Especially if it meant spending the rest of your life in prison."

She spoke with no emotion, as if human life had no worth.

Guy thought of her mother. Of his.

But he could see she was beyond that now. Beyond his appealing to whatever humanity she had left.

"How is it going to happen? Am I going to shoot myself?" His eyes were on the gun she held tightly clasped in her right hand. "Why didn't you kill me in the woods? Why here?"

"You haven't figured it out yet? You'll know soon enough."

She looked around the deserted platform.

"We met on the train. And this is where it will end."

70

The crisscrossing Day-Glo beams of search lights was the first thing Linda saw when she and Pete pulled into the woods.

The second was Guy's SUV.

The sight of the car that he drove back and forth to the train station every day was like a one-two punch. A fact right in front of her eyes that Linda couldn't ignore. Couldn't tell herself that this whole thing was a nightmare she'd wake up from to find her husband asleep next to her in bed.

Not with a two-time killer on the loose and uniformed officers and dogs searching the woods that Guy used to hike through back when he was writing the next great American novel.

Cadaver dogs.

Because they were too late.

Linda spotted Diane Moorland conferring with a detective. She was dressed as usual in a navy power suit with not a hair out of place, except for having traded her trademark high heels for sneakers.

When she saw Linda and Pete, Diane said something to the detective, then walked over to them.

"We don't know how long the car's been here. If it's been parked in the woods all this time."

"No sign of Samantha Hunter?"

Linda knew the answer before Diane shook her head. Her boss gestured to Guy's SUV that the crime scene unit was currently crawling all over.

"A copy of today's newspaper was on top of the car," Diane said. "Paper was open to an article about Stuart Robbins's murder."

Linda said nothing as she tried to process this latest piece of information. She looked at Pete, who was watching the crime scene crew. Then she remembered him telling her that on the night Stuart Robbins was killed, Guy had been thrown out of a downtown Manhattan bar for being drunk.

Mike Bonaker told them that Guy said he didn't remember anything when Bonaker found him on the roof of the abandoned lighthouse staring down at Alfred Johnson's body in the water. In addition to his beaten-up face, Bonaker also said that Guy had been drinking.

Was it possible Guy didn't remember what happened the night Stuart Robbins was killed? And that was why he bought the newspaper?

Did Guy believe he was guilty of Robbins's murder?

Diane's voice was softer as she said, "It's possible that Guy left on his own."

"No." Linda refused to believe that.

"We found something else."

Diane nodded at one of the crime scene techs, who walked over to Linda.

She held something in her gloved hands. "It was on the passenger seat."

Linda recognized it immediately. Guy's book bag. He might abandon the car, but he'd never leave his book bag behind.

Unless—

He was planning to leave everything behind.

The tech had opened the bag and was sliding out a book. One of the early editions from Guy's collection.

Linda had never read the book, but she'd seen a few film and television adaptations and knew how Tolstoy's masterpiece ended.

The Scarsdale train station was only a few miles away.

Linda's mind spun back to Saturday morning when she was awakened by two cops at her front door.

She'd been so sure that something had happened to Guy.

Fearing the worst.

Were those fears about to be realized? Was Guy planning to follow in the footsteps of his mother and Dorothy Miller?

Then she had a thought that cut her to the bone.

Had Guy done it already? Cheating Samantha Hunter of her final revenge?

Something nagged at Linda's mind as she pulled out her phone and Googled the Metro-North schedule.

"What is it?" Pete asked.

Linda waved him off, ignored the questioning look in Diane's eyes.

The crime scene tech was still holding the book.

Linda stared at the title.

Anna Karenina.

That was what was bothering her. The name.

Not Hunter Rellim, the name on the driver's license that had ultimately led Linda to Samantha Hunter's true identity. Another name. The one Ryan overheard her telling Douglas Beldock at the Red Rose Tavern.

She said her name was Anna.

"I know what Samantha Hunter's planning."

71

"**D**o you understand now why I told you my name was Anna?" Her tone was matter-of-fact, the dim light on the platform casting her face in shadow.

"I got the idea from watching you reading on the train. I always sat a few rows behind you. For weeks before we ever spoke."

And Guy had never noticed her.

Then realization dawned. Back in May, he'd been rereading *Anna Karenina*.

He'd planned to give it to her as a gift after she told him her name the morning they stood together in the train well because no seats were available.

The book was in his bag a week later when she came up behind him in Grand Central and asked him to meet her at a bar in the city.

Their whispered conversation next to the bar's restroom that evening was the last time Guy saw her.

Until tonight.

The book was still in his bag.

"Except that in this story, Anna isn't the one who dies."

Her words barely registered. Guy's mind had just gone someplace else.

He was on the roof of the abandoned lighthouse, Dorothy's face lighting up as she unwrapped his birthday gift. It was the Virginia Woolf book. The one that had been missing from his bookcase for so many years.

"I gave Dorothy a book," Guy said. "I wrote something in it."

72

Linda hardly breathed as she and Pete sped along Scarsdale's quiet, late-night streets.

An emergency call to the train dispatcher had offered little comfort.

He told them that even if he could relay the communication to the engineer in time, attempting to stop a train only minutes away wasn't just unlikely. It could be dangerous.

What made it worse was the train was an express to Grand Central, which meant it was traveling at a higher rate of speed and wouldn't slow down as it approached the Scarsdale station.

Linda was positive that that was how Samantha Hunter planned to kill Guy.

She was going to push him onto the tracks. Into the path of an oncoming train. The way the fictional Anna Karenina had died.

And Linda's baby brother, crushed under the wheels of that hit-and-run car.

The train had left the White Plains station at 12:07. It would be passing through Scarsdale at approximately 12:18.

As they followed the Scarsdale PD vehicles driving with their sirens off so as to not alert their target, Linda closed her eyes and did something she hadn't done in decades.

She prayed.

73

S omething in her face had changed again.

Did she know about the Virginia Woolf book? Had Dorothy kept it?

She seemed to be wavering. The hand holding the gun was trembling.

He thought he might be finally getting through.

As they stared at one another, Guy was struck by something familiar in her brown eyes.

Then she shook her head, and the spell was broken.

"You don't get to rewrite the story. You don't get to say you loved her. She didn't jump from that roof because she couldn't live anymore. She jumped because everything precious had been stolen from her. She didn't take her life. All of you did."

Guy saw it then. The emotions she could no longer hide, which he'd caught glimpses of in unguarded moments.

A woman desperate for revenge, so consumed with grief and rage that she killed without compunction.

She tightened her grip on the gun.

"Move!"

74

P ete had barely hit the brakes when Linda pushed open the passenger door and ran from the car.

Even from here, she could see the navy uniforms swarming the platform, weapons raised.

"Linda! What are you doing?"

She ignored Pete.

Ignored Diane, who was also calling her name.

Ignored the voices of the Scarsdale PD officers as she sprinted up the steps, shouting at her to stay back.

She almost lost it when she saw them at the edge of the platform. Samantha Hunter was holding a gun on Guy, her eyes wild.

"Come any closer, and he dies."

"Don't hurt him. Let him go. Please!"

Linda's voice broke on a sob. She saw her husband's brown eyes widen in shock when he saw her.

She started running again, but strong arms grabbed her and held her back.

"What are you doing? Trying to get yourself killed?" Pete whispered fiercely in her ear. "You're an unarmed civilian."

"Let me go."

But Pete held her fast.

"You can't reason with her. She's beyond that now."

Linda tried to wrench free, in her mind's eye seeing Guy's lifeless body.

And Mikey's.

"Drop your weapon," an officer with a megaphone shouted. "It's over."

Samantha Hunter shook her head and grasped the gun tighter.

In the distance, Linda heard the *toot toot!* of the approaching train.

75

The gun was still pointed at his heart.

They were standing so close to the edge Guy could see the tracks below.

It was at least a six-foot drop.

"Don't hurt him. Let him go. Please!"

Guy startled at the sound of his wife's voice.

Linda was here?

"Drop your weapon. It's over."

The cop's voice was nearly drowned out by a shrill whistle.

Anna had heard it too.

The train was coming down the tracks.

In that split second of distraction, Guy saw something out of the corner of his eye.

A cop taking aim.

Guy dove at her legs, a deafening blast of gunfire echoing in his head as they both hit the ground.

Her brown eyes wide with shock were the last thing he saw.

As the bullet tore through him, he heard it.

The ocean's roar.

When he opened his eyes, she was standing there.

At the edge of the roof.

He tried to reach her, but it was as if he was slogging through quicksand. The closer he got, the farther away she seemed.

When he finally made it across, he reached out his arms to pull her back.

He was holding empty air.

Her name was on his lips as he watched her go over, her long, auburn hair flying behind her as she soared through the star-filled night.

76

Mike Bonaker pushed open the door and went inside.

More than a year now since his wife passed, and he still hadn't gotten used to the silence that greeted him every time he walked into his house. He hung up his jacket and went into the kitchen. The dishes from this morning's breakfast were still in the sink.

Bonaker opened the fridge and reached for a beer but changed his mind. He needed something stronger.

In the living room cabinet, he pulled out a shot glass and the bottle of bourbon he kept for special occasions. After he sat down on the sofa, he poured out a shot and closed his eyes as he felt that slow burn easing down his chest and curling through his belly.

He poured another one.

But Dorothy Miller followed him wherever he went.

Would he ever stop seeing her body being pulled from the sea in a tragic replay of what happened forty years ago? When Alfred Johnson was dragged out of the ocean in almost the exact same spot?

Back then, Johnson's widowed mother had to identify her son's body at the morgue.

This time around, that god-awful task fell to Dorothy Miller's only living kin.

But her daughter was too distraught to make the trip from her home in Pikesville, Maryland, around the corner from the house where her mother had lived for almost forty years with her husband.

Until he died two weeks before Dorothy Miller took her own life, right in the middle of the holiday season.

So Bonaker sent Miller's daughter a series of photos taken by the Manatawkett medical examiner. That was followed by her mother's remains, after the coroner released Miller's body following his finding of suicide as the official cause of death.

When Bonaker opened his front door on a frigid February afternoon two months later, for a horrifying moment, he thought Dorothy Miller was standing there. To accuse him of letting all those terrible things happen on his watch.

It was like seeing a ghost. Except that her hair was dark; her eyes brown.

Bonaker saw the deep sorrow in those eyes. The bewilderment. The hurt. The helplessness. And the anger. He understood that anger.

He'd been surprised when she phoned and said she needed to see him. That meant she wanted answers. It made him wonder how much Dorothy Miller had shared with her only child.

He guessed not much, or she wouldn't have called.

What would he tell her?

Miller's daughter had a right to know. But did he want to be the one to bring her more grief?

Bonaker was still wrestling with that when Samantha Hunter showed up and sat across from him in this very room. Looking as if, at any moment, she'd shatter into a dozen pieces, she told him that her father hadn't been cold in his grave when her mother died.

She said she didn't believe that she killed herself. Because she didn't want to believe that her mother would leave her.

Bonaker understood that. Dorothy Miller's death had stolen something from him too.

Then Hunter showed him what she'd brought with her. The real reason for her visit. She said she found it in the back of her mother's closet.

When he opened the shoebox and saw the lone item inside, Bonaker was shocked. When he could speak again, he wanted to know if she'd touched it. He told her that was very important.

Hunter shook her head and said she didn't know what the gold chain meant. Her mother never talked about her past; about growing up in Manatawkett.

"Did it belong to my mother?" she asked.

"I don't think so," he said.

"Whose was it, then? Why did she have it? How did it get broken? Why is there blood on it?"

The questions hung in the air between them.

"Please, I have to know. I have to know why." Her face was full of anguish. *"Did something happen out here?"*

That was when Bonaker saw something else shadowing her eyes.

Guilt.

She spoke in a halting voice.

"My mother and I—we hadn't been in touch a lot in the last few months. I was angry with her because she wouldn't tell me. And I needed

to know. Even though I was also afraid to find out the truth. It was about my father."

He waited, but she didn't say anything more.

"This wasn't your fault," he said at last. Whatever had caused the estrangement between mother and daughter would stay forever between them. But he empathized with her; with how it must feel when someone you loved took their own life.

Toward the end, Ruby had begged him to take her out of her pain. He'd refused.

Had he made the right decision? Bonaker still didn't know.

Samantha Hunter was looking at him expectantly.

Still, Bonaker wrestled with it. He didn't want to lie, but if Miller hadn't seen fit to tell her daughter, she must have had her reasons.

He was under no obligation to tell her. Cops made calls like that all the time.

Except that she wasn't just anyone. She had a right to know what happened to her mother. She deserved the truth.

And still he grappled with it, with the wisdom of telling her.

If she felt his turmoil, she didn't show it because, in the next moment, she got up and put the lid back on the shoebox.

"Where are you going?"

"If you won't tell me, I'll find someone who will."

Bonaker saw it leaving with her, his chance to finally get justice. He didn't realize how badly he wanted it until she picked up the box.

"Wait."

She turned around. Slowly sat back down, the shoebox in her lap.

Then he told her.

Bonaker remembered seeing the dawning horror on her face as he talked. Ending by saying that if they were able to get DNA off of the chain, it could go a long way toward solving the murder of her mother's best friend's boyfriend. The boy who might have witnessed the assault.

He told her that Dorothy Miller had left town without giving a statement. That he knew she was the victim of a gang rape but could never prove it.

Before she walked out of his living room, Bonaker gave Dorothy Miller's daughter three names.

At the time, he had no idea what he'd set in motion.

Or so he'd been telling himself ever since the news about what had taken place at the Scarsdale train station broke.

Samantha Hunter had turned herself into a one-woman avenging army.

Not that that absolved him. Bonaker might as well have been the one who put a loaded weapon in her hand.

He'd wanted the three of them to pay for what they did to Dorothy Miller. And one of them to pay for the murder of Alfred Johnson.

Was the torn chain Miller's suicide note?

Had she wanted her only child to find it in the hope that the chain would find its way to him?

Vengeance from beyond the grave?

No, not vengeance.

Justice.

After all this time.

He got the call an hour ago. The lab in Riverhead had been able to lift DNA off of the broken chain. Afterward, Bonaker sat at his desk in stunned silence. When he could move again, he left the precinct and drove home.

Bonaker looked at the bourbon bottle now, thought about pouring another shot. Hell, maybe he'd polish off the entire bottle. Another way of delaying the inevitable?

With a heavy sigh, he got up from the sofa and took the empty shot glass into the kitchen, where it joined the other dishes in the sink.

As he heard the screen door bang shut after him, Bonaker suddenly felt older than his sixty-five years.

There was one last piece of official police business to take care of before this endless day was done.

77

He found her sitting under a tree at the side of her house.

A few feet away, the framed photos suspended from a large oak knocked gently against each other in the breeze.

August was still a few weeks away, but Bonaker could already detect autumn in the air. The time when living things died.

She looked up as he approached. Except for the gray hair, she hadn't changed much in all these years. Lived on the same street half a mile from Manatawkett Harbor, where she'd grown up. The only child of parents who'd divorced when she was a teenager.

She never married. Worked at the Manatawkett Community Church most of her adult life.

He thought that was how she coped with tragedy, the loss she could never move beyond. Helping others in need. Like the suicide fund she'd started in her best friend's name.

But it was much more than that. It was her way of trying to atone.

He wondered how she lived with it all these years. What lies she told herself in the dead of night when there was nowhere to hide from the reality of what she'd done.

Bonaker felt a surge of anger that had been growing steadily ever since he got the call from the lab.

Nancy Conklin didn't have the right to grieve.

"Afternoon, Mike. What brings you here?"

Her tone was deceptively casual. Instead of answering, Bonaker walked over to the tree whose branches held the photos of Alfred Johnson and Dorothy Miller.

Everyone in town knew about the shrine Conklin had built to honor her dead friends. Now Bonaker saw it for what it was.

This wasn't a legacy to Conklin's departed loved ones; a monument created in Miller and Johnson's memory.

It was here as a constant reminder.

So that she'd never forget.

"Can I offer you something? A glass of lemonade? I've got a batch of fresh-baked gingerbread cookies cooling in the kitchen."

Conklin was famous for her baking skills, her pies and cakes often taking first prize at community bake-offs.

Now he heard the hesitancy in her voice. She knew he wasn't here on a social visit.

Bonaker turned from the tree, away from the photo of Dorothy Miller standing at the bottom of the bluff, dwarfed by the abandoned lighthouse sitting at the top. An image that would now always be with him.

Anger reignited as he reached into his pocket. "I have something to show you."

A wary expression narrowed Conklin's close-set eyes. "What have you got there, Mike?"

When she saw what was inside the plastic evidence envelope, her face turned ashen.

"Do you recognize it?"

She opened her mouth, but no words came out. She shook her head from side to side as if that could somehow ward off the truth, then she turned an uncomprehending gaze on him. "I don't understand."

Bonaker went on as if she hadn't spoken. "Is this the gold chain you told me you gave Alfred Johnson for his high school graduation?"

Conklin still looked shell-shocked as she nodded.

"When I asked you if Alfred Johnson was wearing the chain the night he died, you told me you weren't sure. Is that still your statement?"

She didn't respond right away, sensing a trap. "He might have been. I don't remember. It was a long time ago."

"That's not true. You knew Johnson was wearing it that night. DNA matching yours was found on the chain. You bought it for him, so it would be natural for your DNA to be there. But you must have cut yourself when the chain broke. That's what accounted for the blood on the chain. And blood doesn't lie."

He battled to get his emotions under control. When he could speak again, Bonaker uttered only one word.

"Why?"

Nancy Conklin dragged her gaze from the chain. Now he could see the guilt that had always been there.

She started talking.

78

1984

The bonfire was in full swing when she got there.

It was a beautiful early August night, but Nancy had other things on her mind.

Dorothy was keeping secrets.

She thought Nancy didn't know, but Dorothy couldn't hide anything from her. They'd been best friends since elementary school.

Until Alfred Johnson was invited into their exclusive club.

He was an only child, like Nancy and Dorothy.

And Nancy's secret crush.

She and AJ started dating in junior high. This past June, she bought him a gold chain as a high school graduation gift and to celebrate their future together.

Dorothy would be her maid of honor.

Nancy wondered if anyone had ever died of happiness. All she could think about was marrying AJ, who was sure to propose any day now.

She was already picturing her wedding, shared with the two people she loved most in the world.

Until tonight.

When Nancy didn't see Dorothy at the bonfire, she figured she was with Guy Kingship, whom she'd been secretly meeting on the roof of the abandoned lighthouse for weeks.

Why Dorothy would want to go to that creepy place that was haunted by the ghost of a man who killed himself, Nancy hadn't a clue. And she didn't know why Dorothy was wasting her time with a spoiled city boy who was never going to put a ring on her finger.

Nancy looked around for AJ but didn't see him.

She couldn't stand the way he followed Kingship and his friends around like he had no dignity or pride. That just made her hate Guy Kingship even more.

She wasn't sure why she left the bonfire and started walking.

Nancy was halfway down the beach when she saw Stuart Robbins and Douglas Beldock coming from the direction of the abandoned lighthouse. They were laughing and clapping each other on the back. That was when she got a bad feeling.

She tried to hurry out of their line of vision, but Robbins and Beldock were so drunk they didn't notice her anyway. After they were gone, she continued down the beach, even though a part of her wanted to turn around.

And it wasn't only because the lighthouse spooked her. When she at last got up the nerve to open the door, it was pitch-black inside.

Then she heard something. A grunting sound.

As her eyes accustomed to the darkness, she saw a shadow moving on the wall. Under the stairs.

She took a few steps closer.

AJ was on top of Dorothy.

Dorothy wasn't moving.

For a terrifying second, Nancy thought she was dead.

Then she was running.

Screaming as she tried to pull AJ off of Dorothy, her hands suddenly around his neck, barely aware of the pain when the chain broke and her fingers bled.

And still she hung on, squeezing for all she was worth. AJ grabbed her hands, pushed her so hard that she fell back.

He zipped up his fly as he got unsteadily to his feet.

Letting out a yell, she leapt to her feet and intercepted him as he tried to run for the door. Blocked his way.

He turned and ran in the other direction. Toward the stairs.

She chased him up to the roof. When he pushed open the door, Nancy was right behind him.

She followed him across the roof. He stopped a few feet from the edge. AJ was so tall that the rusting iron railing barely reached his calves.

As he stood there staring down at the ocean, Nancy wondered if he was thinking about jumping.

She couldn't let him do that. He was her whole life. There was no one else. Never had been and never would be again.

She walked over to him. Touched his shoulder.

When he turned around, Nancy saw the bloody red welts on his neck where she'd tried to strangle him with the gold chain she'd bought him for his graduation.

The wounds needed to be cleaned so they could heal. They mustn't be allowed to fester.

Tonight never happened.

That was the only way to move on.

" . . . so sorry . . . forgive me . . ."

She already had.

"Everything's going to be okay," she said, enfolding him in her arms as she crooned the words over and over, like a mantra.

"I didn't mean to do it." His shoulders had begun to heave.

"Shhh . . ."

"I never wanted to hurt her."

He was crying now.

"No more talking."

"Do you think she'll forgive me?"

"That's enough now."

"I couldn't help myself."

"Stop."

"She was just so beautiful."

"Will you please just stop?"

"All I could think was, why should those boys get to have her?"

He was crying harder, his voice muffled against her chest.

But she heard every word.

"After Stu and Doug left, she just lay there staring at me with those big, blue eyes. Like she thought I was going to save her. I wanted to. But I wanted her so badly. I loved her for so long. I thought if I dated you, she might finally start to notice me. But she never gave me the time of day."

He pulled back and swiped at his eyes. "Do you think she'll forgive me?" he repeated. "Nancy?"

She didn't answer. She couldn't.

"You won't tell anyone, right?"

Nancy shook her head. "Don't worry. Your secret's safe with me."

She placed her hands on his shoulders. He looked at her hands, then up at her face. He started to frown, but his feet were already leaving the ground.

"What are you—"

He lost his balance.

Stumbled back.

All she had to do was reach out and grab him, but it was as if she'd turned to stone.

He screamed as he went over, his voice drowned out by the surf.

79

Leaning over, she saw him fly through the air, a stunned look on his face as he flailed his arms in vain. She was still watching when his body hit the water.

At the time, she didn't know she wasn't alone on the roof. All she could think was that she had to get out of there.

When she came back down, Dorothy was still in the corner under the stairs. Her eyes were open now. Nancy avoided her gaze as she pulled her to her feet. With Dorothy leaning heavily on her, she managed to get her out the door.

That was when Nancy saw a waitress and a busboy she knew from the yacht club hurrying up the beach. If she'd left the lighthouse a few minutes earlier, they would have seen her and Dorothy.

Nancy let out a relieved breath. Then fear grabbed her by the throat. Had they witnessed AJ falling from the lighthouse roof?

When the coast was clear, Nancy half walked, half carried Dorothy to her car that was parked across the street from the beach.

She knew she should take Dorothy to the police station, but she panicked. So, instead, she drove home.

Waited for the doorbell to ring.

Was still waiting while she watched the replay of what happened the night before on television Sunday morning. Her mind detached as she watched AJ's body being dragged out of the water and laid on the beach, the crowd of onlookers gaping from the shoreline.

As if what was unfolding in time delay on her TV screen had nothing to do with her.

When the doorbell finally rang later that morning, it wasn't because she was about to be arrested.

Mike Bonaker needed her help because AJ had been her boyfriend, and Nancy was the closest person to AJ outside of his mother.

Nancy hadn't seen the gold chain again after she chased AJ up to the lighthouse roof. When Bonaker described the welts and bruises on AJ's neck, she covered for herself by telling him she wasn't sure if AJ had been wearing the gold chain she'd bought him for his high school gradation the night before.

She also told Bonaker that she'd seen Stuart Robbins and Douglas Beldock walking down the beach away from the lighthouse after AJ's body went off the roof, which was a lie. She told him they raped Dorothy, which wasn't a lie. She'd learned that from AJ before he plunged to his death.

Bonaker looked shocked when he heard about the gang rape. He assumed that Nancy had been told about the assault from Dorothy, who still hadn't spoken.

Then he told her that someone had been arrested for AJ's murder.

After Bonaker left, Dorothy came out of her bedroom. She said they had to tell Sergeant Bonaker what happened. She was afraid that the boy Bonaker had arrested was Guy Kingship. After Stuart Robbins beat up Kingship, he'd left him unconscious on the lighthouse roof.

That was when Nancy realized that Kingship had been on the roof when AJ went off of the edge.

"We can't let an innocent person take the blame." Dorothy had finally found her voice.

Nancy stared at her as if she'd lost her mind. "Are you crazy? You want me to go to jail?"

Dorothy shook her head. "You were trying to stop him. Whatever happened up there was an accident."

"So AJ just happened to fall off the roof? After I caught my boyfriend raping my best friend. Who's going to believe that?"

Dorothy's eyes were imploring. "We have to tell the truth. Don't you see? It's the only way."

"Really? My parents and everyone in town will know that the boy I planned to marry was a monster!"

"We can't let Guy go to prison for something he didn't do."

"But you want me to go. Kingship's the one who deserves to be punished. If he and his friends hadn't taken what didn't belong to them, AJ would still be alive."

"That's not true."

"Oh yeah? What do you think will happen now? Kingship will marry you and you'll live happily ever after? You know that's just a fairy tale. His father would never allow it. We're good enough to screw but not to be seen in public. That's why Kingship made you keep your relationship a secret. He was ashamed of you."

"You're wrong. He loves me."

But Nancy could hear the uncertainty in her voice.

And how could someone with Dorothy's background even know what love was?

When she left the living room, Nancy followed her back into her bedroom and watched Dorothy open her closet and pull out a dress.

"Where are you going?"

"To the police station."

"Don't do this."

Dorothy started to get dressed.

"I gave you a place to live. After your mother threw you out and half the town thought you were sleeping with your stepfather."

Dorothy's face tightened, but she said nothing as she walked to the bureau and put her keys in her pocketbook.

"If you go to the police, I'll say that you asked for it. You're just a tramp, like everyone says. Seducing all the men in town. You were the one who killed AJ to stop him from spreading it around. I was never there."

"Yes, you were. I have the proof."

Nancy looked at Dorothy in horror. Then she held out her hand. "Give it to me. Give me the chain. It's mine. It belongs to me."

Dorothy shook her head.

"Please, Dorothy. We've been best friends since the third grade. We have to stick together now. I'm begging you. Don't send me to prison."

Nancy started to cry.

After a moment, Dorothy sat down on the bed and took off her shoes. Then she lay down and closed her eyes.

The next day, Nancy heard that the charges had been dropped.

The boy in custody was released. No one else was arrested.

Dorothy never spoke another word to her.

Three weeks later, she left Manatawkett.

Nancy never saw her again.

80

After Conklin finished, she turned a stricken face to him.

"Is that why Dorothy came back to Manatawkett to kill herself? Jumping off the lighthouse roof was her revenge? Her way of punishing me?"

Bonaker didn't answer right away. He was still in shock. Not only because of what Nancy Conklin had done but also because of the crime Alfred Johnson had committed.

"This wasn't about payback," he finally said, anger once again heating his voice. "That's what you don't understand. It was about her. The despair she felt. Because of the secret she was forced to keep all these years. And her guilt for her role in covering up your crime."

Conklin had used Dorothy Miller's victimization by her stepfather to blackmail her into keeping silent. Was there no end to Nancy Conklin's evil?

"Don't look at me like that. It's not as if you're so lily-white." Before he could ask what she meant, Conklin went on. "If back then I'd told you what happened, would you have arrested me?"

His silence was her answer.

"That's what I thought. I'm not sure I'm even remembering it right. The whole thing happened such a long time ago. I was so angry, which anyone would understand. I didn't mean for AJ to die. That wasn't what I wanted."

"Wasn't it?" Bonaker shook his head. "You can lie to yourself all you like, but we both know you pushed him off the lighthouse roof. But it doesn't matter what I think. That's for a jury to decide. Tell me, Nancy. Was it worth it?"

She didn't answer. She cocked her head as she gazed up at him, a crafty look coming into her eyes. "One thing I know for sure. Dorothy left Manatawkett with AJ's gold chain. How did you end up with it?"

Bonaker's jaw tightened.

"Dorothy Miller's daughter brought it to me. She didn't want to believe that her mother had killed herself. She was looking for answers."

"Why do you think Dorothy waited all this time? Forty-year anniversary?"

"That's something we'll never know."

She flinched at the censure in his voice. "How dare you sit in judgment of me!"

They stared at one another for an interminable moment.

"What else did you tell Dorothy's daughter?"

"That isn't any business of yours. It's not why I'm here."

"Isn't it?"

Bonaker's eyes didn't quite meet hers, but he was sure Conklin saw the guilt he couldn't hide. She should know what it looked like. She'd been living with her own guilt all these years.

"Then maybe you can answer this question," Conklin said. "If Dorothy told her daughter what happened at the lighthouse that night, why did Samantha Hunter go after all three of them?"

When Bonaker didn't respond, Conklin went on. "I didn't know Guy Kingship was on the lighthouse roof that night. You gave Dorothy's daughter his name. Why else would she have thought he was part of it?" Her eyes blazed with triumph. "You had to believe that Kingship was one of the rapists because he was the only one on the roof when you got there. Otherwise, he would have had no reason to kill AJ."

Bonaker said nothing. He couldn't dispute the truth of what she said, remembering how the witnessed altercation between Kingship and Johnson in front of the lighthouse had helped to bolster his theory of what happened that night.

As if reading his mind, Conklin said, "You needed Kingship to build your case against the hated city boys."

Which fell apart after Bonaker was forced to let Guy Kingship go.

"What about you?" he shot back, even though he knew that, once again, she'd spoken the truth. But he wasn't the only one in town with a bias against the summer people. "For years, you told anyone who would listen that three boys from New York raped your best friend. And one of them killed your boyfriend because Johnson was in the wrong place at the wrong time. All smoke and mirrors to throw folks off so they wouldn't know who the real killer was."

Conklin shook her head. "You can't blame me for everything. And you're the one who's blowing smoke. The truth is, I never mentioned Guy Kingship's name to you."

"But by your own admission, you lied when you said you saw Robbins and Beldock walking away from the lighthouse after Johnson went off the roof," Bonaker said, anger once again slamming through him. "You couldn't have seen them then because you were in your car driving home with Dorothy Miller. After you killed Alfred Johnson."

"I didn't lie about seeing Robbins and Beldock. I just told you it happened later. I didn't know then that Guy Kingship was on the roof that night."

"If you had known, you wouldn't have had to lie about when you saw Robbins and Beldock because you'd have had Kingship to blame for Johnson's death."

"Is what you did any different? Maybe you're the one who's in denial. The one kidding himself. You wanted justice. Or maybe it was revenge. Tell me"—she threw his own words back at him—"was it worth it?"

When he didn't answer, she said in a voice that was barely above a whisper, "I guess we both have blood on our hands."

Another silence fell. This one seemed to stretch on forever. Then Bonaker reached into his back pocket and pulled out a pair of handcuffs.

Conklin rose from the bench and placed a hand on the small of her back as she stretched. "Are those really necessary? You don't have to worry, Mike. I'm not planning to run. Aside from being a fugitive at my age, where would I go?"

She walked over to the oak tree that held the framed photos. "Is it okay if I take a few things with me?"

"Afraid I can't let you do that."

Conklin nodded as if it was the response she expected, then turned back to the tree.

She studied each photo, as if committing the images to memory. Her gaze lingered on the shot of Dorothy posing in front of the ocean in a red-and-black bikini, smiling as she waved to the camera.

"Ready?"

Conklin didn't answer as she walked away from the tree. Bonaker followed her to the front of the house. On the porch, she leaned down and inspected the geraniums that appeared to be freshly cut. The soil in the urn still looked damp, but Bonaker doubted that the flowers would survive more than a few days without water.

Bonaker watched her as she took one last look around.

At the rocking chair where he'd sometimes see her sitting alone at night when he drove past her house.

The swing that he'd rarely seen anyone occupy.

Conklin looked back at the house, frowning as if she'd forgotten something. Slipping a key from underneath one of the urns, she locked the front door.

Bonaker wondered why. Out of habit, he guessed. It seemed fitting, somehow. Gave a finality to things.

A breeze was coming off of the water, and Nancy Conklin looked to the west for a last glimpse of Manatawkett Harbor.

Then Mike Bonaker took her arm and escorted her down the three steps of her front porch to the police cruiser that waited in the driveway.

81

"That's the last one."

Linda watched Pete finish taping the box and add it to the others strewn across the floor.

The office at One Hogan Place had been her second home for almost fifteen years. She tried to ignore the ache in her lower back as she reached for a box to start loading onto the dolly sitting by the door.

He grabbed it from her. "I've got this."

"You have to let me do something."

"You need your rest. Sit down. Take a load off your feet."

"I'm not an invalid, you know."

But she did as she was told and went over to the butterscotch sofa that sat in front of the window. It did feel better being off of her feet. Although she was still in the first trimester of her pregnancy, the stress of the past few weeks had started to catch up with her. The physical exertion of packing up her office was proving more strenuous than she'd anticipated.

"Thanks, Pete."

It seemed lately that she was always thanking him for something. Once he finished loading the boxes, all that would be left was to transport everything to her car that was sitting in the designated parking space she'd had for years.

"Hungry?" Pete asked. Linda shook her head. "Thirsty?" He went over to the mini refrigerator behind her desk and pulled out a water bottle. "You need to stay hydrated."

Linda had to smile as he handed her the bottle. For the past three weeks, he hadn't stopped fussing over her. He texted her half a dozen times a day and seemed to always find an excuse to stop by her office or her house. She had to admit, she was grateful for the company.

"That's it." Pete wiped his brow, then joined her on the sofa.

Linda took a swig from the water bottle and looked around her office. The place looked so bare with all her case files that had taken up nearly half the space gone. And the bookcase against the far wall now had several empty shelves. Her legal tomes alone filled three boxes.

She wondered where she'd store them. There wasn't a lot of room on the bookshelf in her basement office, and very little space on the bookcase in the living room that held Guy's classics collection.

Linda turned her head away; she didn't want Pete to see her tearing up. She could never predict when the feelings would hit, often at the most inopportune moments.

"You can always say you changed your mind. Diane would take you back in a heartbeat."

He thought she was rethinking her decision.

"Or consider extending your maternity leave. Give you more time to decide what you want to do."

Her boss had made the offer after Linda informed her that she was resigning.

Linda shook her head. She no longer had the stomach for the law. She wasn't sure she even knew what justice looked like anymore.

"You have to stop blaming yourself, Linda. You did everything you could."

Did she? In her mind, the jury was still out.

"You know better than anyone that the Manhattan DA will never accept a plea," Pete said. "Samantha Hunter's going to spend the rest of her life in prison."

That was part of the problem. Linda wanted to hate her. Had spent the last two weeks trying to hate her. But when she watched the arraignment from the back of the overflowing courtroom at 100 Centre Street, the defendant sitting silent and ramrod straight next to her public defender, all Linda saw was another victim.

She'd known others like Samantha Hunter. Had prosecuted a few.

One the father of a rape victim who'd killed herself. Shot his daughter's rapist dead on the courthouse steps after the jury let him walk.

It could have been anyone.

A father. A husband.

A daughter.

Burning up with so much pain and rage that they took the law into their own hands.

Wasn't that one of the reasons that she became a prosecutor? To get justice within the parameters of the law? Smug in her certainty that every rapist and murderer was guilty?

Like Frida Colmann's husband. Like the hit-and-run driver who killed her brother. It was also her way of trying to expiate her own guilt.

Who was she kidding? All she'd ended up doing was exchanging one form of vengeance for another.

"Do you think Guy knew who she was?" Pete asked.

Linda had been wondering about that too. The investigation was still ongoing, but so far there was no evidence that Guy had known Samantha Hunter's true identity.

A search of her home computer had revealed a damning trail of breadcrumbs that told the whole story of her murderous vendetta.

It turned out that Samantha Hunter hadn't sat down next to Guy at a bar. They met on the Metro-North. Which in her mind had made the Scarsdale train station the ideal crime scene. The perfect place to pull off the last murder.

Her endgame.

"Ready to roll?"

Linda nodded and let Pete help her to her feet.

While he wheeled the dolly through the doorway, she took one last look around. Then she picked up her bag and jacket and followed him into the hall.

◆

After Pete had gone, the house felt as quiet as a grave.

They'd spent the last several hours in the basement, unpacking the boxes. When they were finished, Linda invited him to stay for dinner. But he said he had plans. This was Saturday night, after all. It wasn't as if they were a couple. They were colleagues and friends, although the colleague part had officially ended.

And they weren't lovers.

She remembered calling him the morning the two NYPD detectives first showed up looking for Guy and hearing a female voice in the background.

Pete had a life. She had no claim on him.

Don't be a stranger were Pete's last words to her before he leaned in and gave her a chaste kiss on the cheek. Then he left, and Linda was alone in an empty house, where the silence felt like an accusation.

She stood in the kitchen now, debating what to make for dinner. Her appetite was still spotty, but she had to eat. The easiest thing would be to microwave a frozen dinner. Or she could defrost a steak for the grill.

That reminded her of all the nights she and Guy had shared barbecued dinners on the patio.

Everything reminded her of him.

Tomorrow was Sunday. She'd drive there in the morning. She visited almost every day.

In the end, she settled for a ham and cheese sandwich.

Linda was taking her plate to the table when she heard something thud against the front door.

82

When she stepped outside, a package was sitting on the porch. Linda didn't recognize the name of the sender, but a portion of the return address was familiar.

Pikesville, Maryland, had been the city and state on Samantha Hunter's fraudulent driver's license.

Linda hadn't seen the street address before. 1601 Reisterstown Road.

Back in the house, she sliced open the paper. Inside the package was an envelope and a book. The envelope contained a handwritten note from someone named Carole Allen.

Allen found the book while cleaning out Dorothy's house in preparation for putting her home up for sale. She hadn't known the complete identity of the book's original owner until she saw his name on the news.

Allen thought he would like to have the book back. She also realized that it was an early edition and might be valuable.

And there was an inscription.

Linda brought the book into the living room. She settled herself in Guy's easy chair and opened to the inside page.

August 6, 1984

To D,

When we met, I knew I'd found my soulmate.

You are the love of my life and always will be.

Yours forever,

Guy

Tears filled her eyes as she read the words her husband had written forty years ago.

If she needed proof that Guy had loved Dorothy Miller, here it was.

And Miller had loved him. Or why would she have kept the book all those years?

Linda's heart went out to her. Victimized first by her stepfather, then by her rapists. And, in the end, by her best friend.

Linda thought about the tragedies that could have been avoided if Miller had told the truth.

Stuart Robbins and Douglas Beldock would have gone to prison, along with Nancy Conklin, who was finally getting the punishment she deserved.

As Linda suspected, Conklin had been guilty of murder. She'd just been wrong about who the victim was.

It was Nancy Conklin who pushed Alfred Johnson off of the roof of the abandoned lighthouse.

The third rapist.

The hidden one.

Conklin repeated the lie that Guy killed Johnson to herself for so long that she became convinced it was the truth.

If it weren't for Nancy Conklin, Dorothy Miller would still be alive. She might have ended up staying in Manatawkett and had her baby there.

Was that the reason Miller left Manatawkett? Why she never gave a statement?

No one knew that Miller had been pregnant when she left town in '84. And her secret might have stayed buried forever if it weren't for the evidence that Samantha Hunter brought to Mike Bonaker after her mother's death.

Who had a lot to answer for himself.

Someone told Samantha Hunter that Robbins, Beldock, and Guy raped her mother. It couldn't have been Dorothy Miller because Guy wasn't one of her attackers.

Linda's money was on Bonaker.

And more information had come to light. The DNA that had been recovered on Alfred Johnson's torn chain belonged to three people.

Nancy Conklin.

Alfred Johnson.

And Dorothy Miller.

Technicians got a hit on DNA that had recently been added to the state's data base.

DNA belonging to Samantha Hunter.

Because Dorothy Miller was her mother.

But there was another familial match.

To Alfred Johnson.

Nancy Conklin had killed her boyfriend and the father of her best friend's child.

Linda could understand why Dorothy Miller hadn't told her daughter. No child wanted to know that she was the product of a rape.

As Linda rose to her feet, her mind started spinning what-ifs.

If Miller hadn't been assaulted, would she and Guy have gotten married? Had a family?

Her heart heavy, Linda walked over to the bookcase. The books were arranged alphabetically by author.

There was an empty space on the bottom shelf, next to the other books by Rachel Kingship's favorite author. The Virginia Woolf book had been missing for decades, Guy unable to recall what happened to it.

Tears once again stung Linda's eyes as she returned *To the Lighthouse* to its rightful place on the bookcase, just below a book that she'd put back on the shelf above.

Anna Karenina.

Would she ever stop reliving the final moments of that terrible night?

The train coming down the tracks.

An officer opening fire.

Guy tackling Samantha Hunter to the ground.

Hearing herself scream as blood blossomed on the back of his shirt.

Guy and Hunter being pulled back from the edge as the train bore down on them.

Barely hearing the screech of brakes as she raced across the platform.

Samantha Hunter being read her Miranda warning and taken away in handcuffs.

Guy lying stiff and unmoving on the platform.

Standing helplessly by as paramedics attempted to revive him and stanch the blood he was losing at an alarming rate.

The whirring of rotor blades in the sky signaling the arrival of the helicopter that would airlift Guy to the nearest hospital . . .

That was three weeks ago. Guy was still there.

He'd been extremely lucky. He survived a bullet to the back. But there were complications. The bullet that had lodged between his shoulder blades broke off inside his body. That led to several surgeries to extract the bullet before it splintered further and damaged vital organs.

Internal bleeding was the doctors' greatest concern, resulting in transfusions that left Guy weak and in the intensive care unit for days.

Doctors were also worried about infection and possible paralysis.

The list of life-threatening possibilities seemed endless.

Then, just as Guy was about to be transferred out of ICU, he lost consciousness. The doctors blamed it on his severe blood loss.

Linda read everything she could find about documented cases where coma patients awakened—in some rare cases, months and even years later.

Guy had been unconscious for almost a week.

She tried to take comfort in the fact that her husband was a hero.

He couldn't save his mother. Or Dorothy Miller.

But he took a bullet for Miller's child.

It was an ending Guy might have written.

But Linda refused to believe that this was the end of their story.

◆

Two days later, as she sat at his bedside, listening to the hiss and beep of machines helping him to breathe, she felt Guy's hand tighten in hers.

She thought she was dreaming when he opened his eyes.

His lips moved.

He whispered her name.

Three Months Later . . .

Most of Manatawkett had turned out for the spectacle.

There had been signs broadcasting the news for the past month, along with articles in the local papers and posts on social media. Nothing was going to keep folks away, not even the unseasonably chilly autumn afternoon, with wind gusts predicted to top thirty miles an hour come the evening.

If a bone-chilling, late December night hadn't stopped people from hurrying to the beach ten months ago to watch a body being dragged from the ocean, the weather wouldn't be a deterrent now.

And it wasn't every day that one had the chance to watch history in the making. For the crowd gathered at the bottom of the cordoned-off bluff, today's event was something they weren't likely to see again in their lifetimes.

It wasn't as if other places throughout America hadn't borne witness to similar, human-engineered devastation over the decades. In fact, there was a controversy going on right now in a neighboring town.

If the crumbling lighthouse that had stood on another eastern bluff for a hundred and fifty years wasn't torn down soon, it would end up being demolition by neglect.

What was happening today was long overdue. And, naturally, it divided the townsfolk.

There were those who were dead-set against the abandoned lighthouse being destroyed. Preservationists and members of the Manatawkett Historical Society thought the 111-foot structure should be designated a landmark that was an integral part of their eastern hamlet. They railed against seeing it demolished, despite the tragic history. They argued that a lost lighthouse was a lost piece of history.

There was another, more personal reason for keeping her standing. It would ensure that no one would forget what happened up there.

Others saw the lighthouse as a place of death, and not just because of her physical deterioration. They hoped that what was about to happen here would bring long-awaited closure. An end to the cycle of violence that had begun with the suicide of the original lighthouse keeper and gone on to claim two more lives.

Whatever side of the ledger folks sat on, no one could disagree that this was a sad day in Manatawkett.

The tragedy of it was, while the '84 murder had at long last been brought to resolution, the identity of the killer had sent shock waves through the community.

Like the victims, the killer was one of their own.

That made it even harder to accept. And forgive.

Her name had immediately been taken off the charities she'd helped manage, including the suicide fund she started in the third victim's memory.

Some laid blame at their own doors, asking themselves how a murderer in their midst could have gone undetected for so long. Conveniently forgetting all the decades of altruistic work she'd done, wiped out the moment news of her arrest swept through the community.

The reverend of the Manatawkett Community Church asked parishioners to pray for her soul. And for the souls of the two victims, who'd left no family behind.

Except the child who belonged to both of them.

That revelation had sent more shock waves through the unincorporated hamlet. Some saw the daughter as the last victim, bringing a sorrowful conclusion to a tragic story.

An open-roof car bearing a miniature replica of an American flag on its windshield was driving onto the sand.

The mayor had arrived.

He was followed by cars containing his entourage, including the deputy mayor, members of the Village Police Benevolent Association, a dizzying collection of district assemblymen, county executives, and other political notables and wannabes.

The mayor lavished a dazzling "vote for me" smile on the crowd behind the rope. He gave a brisk nod to Manatawkett's longtime medical examiner, now using a wheelchair, and a slower nod to Manatawkett's widowed police chief, who stood next to the medical examiner and whose adult daughter—a nurse—stood on her father's other side.

The chief of police was the one who'd made the arrest. Same as he did forty years ago.

Even those who remembered—Jed Whalen and Hank Bistrian, to name two, and Jesse Edwards, who wasn't here and, it was whispered, wasn't long for this world—never knew the name of the boy who'd been charged with the '84 murder.

Not until they saw it on the news.

As people had long suspected, the arrested boy had been from New York City. One of the summer kids, who ended up nearly losing his life because of the snowball effect of a single lie and a conspiracy of silence that came home to roost forty years later.

There were some rumormongers who went so far as to insinuate that the chief of police had gone after his own justice. Others held their tongues, all too aware of the damage that could be done with the vicious spreading of innuendo and gossip.

There was always plenty of blame to go around, and pointing fingers wasn't going to bring back the dead.

At the top of the bluff, bulldozers and dump trucks were moving into position.

A murmur rose up from the crowd.

Children sat on the shoulders of their parents, who craned their necks for the first glimpse of the fireworks that were about to start.

Everyone held their collective breath as the countdown began. When it came, the explosion shook the ground. It felt as if the earth itself had opened.

The bottom went first.

Now the center was going, the band of brown around her middle disappearing.

Sparks of flame shot to the top as she imploded in on herself.

The roof was still intact.

Another deafening blast ripped through her.

And still the roof refused to burn.

Folks looked at one another.

God showing His hand?

The black lantern at the top shattered as the roof finally started to crumble.

As the last of the lighthouse dissolved to earth, she lit up from the inside, like a Fourth of July firecracker.

Then she gave one last gasp, shuddered, and was still.

No one spoke after the tremors died down. Everyone stared at the towering mass of rubble at the top of the bluff. All had stupefied looks on their faces.

The ground trembled with one final aftershock.

After a while, the crowd began to disperse. The spectacle was over. All that was left now was an empty bluff where, for more than a century, the old lighthouse had stood.

Once the rubble and debris were cleared away, it would be as if the lighthouse had never been there. Never existed.

But the Manatawkett skyline was altered forever.

The wind had begun to pick up. The ocean was growing louder, the whitecaps rising higher. The seagulls who'd scattered in the wake of the explosion returned, circling around the top of the bluff as they'd done for centuries, and would continue to do long after the rest of us were gone.

Their mournful cries drowned out by the relentless march of the sea and the pounding of the waves as they crashed into shore.

ACKNOWLEDGEMENTS

On my desk next to my laptop is a framed photo containing three words: FINISHING THE HAT That's a song memorialized by the painter George Seurat in Stephen Sondheim's *Sunday in the Park with George*. Writing can be a lonely, exhilarating, worth-every-second experience. I feel fortunate to have an incredible team in my corner.

The Man on the Train wouldn't exist in its current incarnation if it weren't for my incomparable editor Luisa Smith, who saw all the possibilities for this novel. A debt of gratitude to publisher Charles Perry, whose love of books is inspiring and designed a hell of a cover for this one. What can I say about CEO Otto Penzler, who took a chance on me with my debut novel *Saving Grace*, and has been a staunch advocate ever since? Heartfelt thanks to Julia O'Connell for helping readers get to know us. To Will Luckman and his copy-editing team; and the rest of the gang at Scarlet Books, Penzler Publishers, Mysterious Press, and Ryan Lee Gilbert at the Mysterious Bookshop.

I wouldn't be the writer I am without the Master of Suspense. Growing up watching the films of Alfred Hitchcock taught me how to tell a story cinematically. If you can see that train hurtling down the tracks, you can write it.

A shout-out to my literary agent Doug Grad for his knowledge of lighthouses and expensive sports cars circa 1984.

Thank you to the authors and reviewers who gave the book early endorsements. To the podcasters, interviewers, and organizations like International Thriller Writers, Sisters in Crime, and Mystery Writers of America who create a nurturing community for authors. Friends new and old, who have been steadfast supporters. You know who you are.

My profound appreciation goes to the libraries in New York and Florida who have hosted me. You transform every book lover's life by opening our minds and hearts to the endless possibilities of the written word.

To my husband Ted, who doesn't just make sure I get the legal details right. He's my creative collaborator and always knew where this book was going. Thank you, Ted, for being my life partner.

And lastly, where would we authors be without our readers who make our stories and characters live beyond the page. Thank you from the bottom of my heart!

"Look, I made a hat. Where there never was a hat."